A LITTLE NOBLE

JANET R. MACREERY

outskirts
press

Outskirts Press, Inc.
http://www.outskirtspress.com

ISBN: 978-1-9772-2835-2

Library of Congress Control Number: 2020910470

Cover Photo © 2020 www.gettyimages.com.. All rights reserved - used with permission.

Outskirts Press and the "OP" logo are trademarks belonging to Outskirts Press, Inc.

PRINTED IN THE UNITED STATES OF AMERICA

dedicated to my family
by blood
by marriage
by choice

Chapter One

We had set out from London more than a month ago and I still did not know our exact destination. Travel in a rickety, hired carriage with squeaky wheels was unpleasant and boring. My chaperone, Mr. Willicks, failed as a travel companion. He spoke few words as the two of us bumped through the Scottish countryside. Instead, he read. Plus, he always smelled of cheese.

"Where exactly are we going?" I asked.

No response.

"We are in Scotland, correct? Where will I meet my contact?" Silence. "When we will arrive, then?"

Mr. Willicks did not look up from his papers before he spoke.

"Soon."

Utterly aggravating.

A red and black butterfly fluttered by the carriage's open window. As it flew out of sight the carriage jolted to the right with surprising violence. I grabbed the side of the door for balance and looked over at my chaperone. His scowl expressed annoyance. Another more vicious motion shifted the carriage sideways in the opposite direction. A thunderous snapping noise startled me and I screamed. The horse whinnied a frightening sound and then we were turning end over end. The carriage shuddered as pieces of it broke off and hurled in all directions. The power of the tumble flung my body from one part of the carriage to another. My back slammed into the ceiling then my chin knocked on the seat as my stomach banged against the few remaining floor boards. The last glimpse I had of Mr. Willicks did not comfort me. His face had turned white with fear. Then, my world went black.

The smell brought me to wakefulness. The horrid, acrid smell of burning flesh and hair. Moments passed before I thought to check if it was any part of me that was on fire. It was not. At least not anymore. The ends of my hair were singed and my clothes torn with a few scorch marks present but my cloak was still attached. All in all, it was a small bit of damage.

The strong, beautiful horse who had pulled our feeble carriage had not been so lucky. His body had been lit aflame and continued to burn. The size and smell of the burning pile of rubble indicated it was the horse and nothing else. The driver was nowhere to be seen. Large chunks of our rented carriage lay around my landing spot.

As my head cleared, I gazed up at the tall trees and tried to think back on the happenings that had landed me in my present circumstances. The carriage had separated from the horse and broken apart as it tumbled before coming to its ultimate cessation. I must have been struck in the head by flying debris and knocked unconscious because I could not recall what started the fire. Perhaps the lanterns on the outer sides of the coach became dislodged setting their flames free?

I turned to ask my chaperone what we would do next and realized his absence. My heartbeat quickened and fear pricked up my spine.

"Mr. Willicks?" I called. The only responses were the continuous chirping, whirring, and clicking from (what I hoped) were tiny creatures living in the area. I called out a few more times, each a bit louder to the same result. It would be improper to scream and worthless, as well. He was gone or dead. Possibly both.

"MR. WILLICKS!"

Desperate times cause even the most proper people to do odd things. My screams were met with the briefest moment of silence then a splash, indicating an animal entering nearby water, and the insect concert resumed.

A sense of fear and uncertainty intensified in my chest. I had no idea how long I had been knocked out. Perhaps Mr. Willicks left to seek help? Surely he would return soon with a suitable physician and a new carriage, horse, and driver. Yes. Yes. A professional chaperone would not abandon his charge in the wilderness during an important journey. After all, I had a deadline to meet.

Comfortable with my new idea of where Mr. Willicks had gone, I needed to take stock of my belongings and see if anything essential had burned or was otherwise damaged. The winds had shifted and the dreadful smells now wafted in another direction, away from me. I did not want to think about the animals who would now catch the scents. Animals in the wilds of Scotland, like the rats and other large vermin back home in the streets of London, would not be repulsed by burning flesh as I was. It would attract them.

I studied the jumble of objects and spied my journey trunk. Or what was left of it. Eager to assess the destruction, I reached out to grab it when a sharp pain pierced my stomach. I must have yelled out in pain because birds in a nearby bush flapped and squawked as they took to the sky. My mind catalogued the ways I could treat the cause of the stabbing pain. At worst and least likely, a displaced piece of the carriage had skewered into my belly which would take someone with a greater healing gift than mine. The other possibilities I imagined were not much more comforting but possible to cure. There was one way to know for certain. Look.

Exposing my underskirts anywhere but the privacy of my own home was an assault on common decency. With no one around and the pain getting stronger, I did not see I had a choice. I first established I had not been impaled, which I considered to be good news. Next I could note no blood spots on my cloak which was quite a relief as it meant blood had not seeped through all the layers of my clothing. Moving the strap of my small satchel aside, I folded each layer back one at a time in neat pleats, cloak, bodice, stay, skirts, pockets, under-skirts, until I noticed a speck of blood on my shift. The blood stain was small and did not indicate a great harm. No need to panic. I began the process of returning my clothes to their proper positions and to think about where I could find the plants I needed when I heard a noise from behind me.

"Uh-hem. Pardon me, miss. Do you need help?"

I turned at the sound of a young man's voice, shocked, instantly ashamed for having had my skirts up in public, and yet relieved to see another person. How long had he been standing there? How much had he seen?

"Miss? Are you injured?"

He appeared to be around my age, thirteen or fourteen years old. He continued to walk toward me. I shifted my position to square up my shoulders with his.

"Miss? Do you speak English?"

"Of course I speak English, you dolt!" Realizing my response could anger a potential savage, I got to my feet with as much grace as I could muster. It was a difficult task whilst standing among the rubble of one's travel party.

"You weren't answering so I thought you didn't understand me."

"I understood you perfectly! What I do not understand is why you snuck up on me like a wolf. What do you want?" I made a big show of straightening my skirts, as if I had any dignity left.

He looked confused as I waited for him to speak. Instead, he turned around and walked in the opposite direction.

"Where are you going?" I demanded.

He stopped and turned to face me again.

"You did not seem to want my help. I was leaving you alone."

"No!" I responded a little louder than I had intended. Getting better control of my voice, I continued, "I would appreciate some assistance."

"Right," he said. "Are you injured?"

"I appear to be relatively unharmed, thank you."

"Glad to hear it," he said in a bit of mumble. "How can I help you?"

How could he help me? A good question. I took some time to consider it.

"Where am I?" It was as good a place to start as any.

"You don't know where you are? Are you sure you didn't bump your head?"

"My head is perfectly sound. Do you know where we are?"

"Loch Eirann," he replied as if that would mean something to me. I stood still and silent so he continued. "It's a big lake. Where were you headed?"

"Why?"

"Why would you ask me why?" he demanded.

"I am not in the habit of telling strange young men who skulk in the wilderness my personal business."

"Well, are you in the habit of being stranded by yourself in the middle of a carriage wreck in the wilderness?"

"I suppose not."

"Right. Again I ask, where are you going? I can tell you how far you are from your destination."

I glanced down at the scene around me. My belongings lay about me in the dark browns and blacks of the carriage pieces and busted luggage. I glanced over my shoulder in the direction of what apparently was a big lake. Turning back to the Scotsman, I sighed.

"I do not know."

"If you don't want my help, fine. I'll go."

"No, wait! I do not know my exact destination. Mr. Willicks, my chaperone, did not think it was information I needed to have so he did not tell me."

He closed his eyes and shook his head. With his next breath he stepped up to the mess, picking through the broken pieces of wood and metal and fabric and leather with relative ease.

"Stop that! Are you ransacking my things?"

"Aye, yeah. Whatever Willicks left, too."

"You admit you are stealing from us right in front of me?"

"Yes. No. I'm not stealing. I'm trying to help you recover anything useful, like money."

"Oh," I said. "That makes sense."

He was bent over, combing through wreckage, so I cannot be sure, but it sounded as if he muttered something like, "thank you for your approval."

"Where did Willicks keep the cash?"

My eyes flashed to the remnants of my chaperone's trunk for the briefest moment but the Scotsman caught it.

"I'm not here to rob you," he said as he pulled a knife from his sock.

I stared at him, my body tense with a fresh flash of fear. Sweat dampened my hands and back. He sliced the knife through the fabric lining of Mr. Willicks's trunk and I relaxed a bit. He pulled out a small sack cinched tight and tied with a thin leather strap, opened it to peer inside, and closed it again.

"Let's start over," he said. "I'm Calum."

Chapter Two

"Good day, Mr. Calum. I am Mercy Laroche."

"Calum. Not Mr. Calum."

"Fine. Good day, Calum."

"Right. How can I help you get on your way?"

I pondered my options. It did not take long as I was unaware of any options available to me. Even fewer now that Calum had possession of the travel money. At least he had returned his knife to its resting place.

"Do you have any suggestions, Calum?"

He let out quite an audible sigh and rubbed his hand on his forehead.

"Since you don't know where you are going, why don't you tell me where you have been? Where did your journey begin?"

"We started out from home weeks ago, now," I told Calum.

"Where is home?" he asked.

"That is quite rude," I told him.

"What? Asking you where you started out from?"

"Interrupting me to ask a question is rude."

Calum rubbed his forehead even harder and let out a louder sigh.

"Do you want my help or not?"

"Why do you keep asking me? Of course, I want your help, however, you need not be rude while you assist me."

"Right." He put his hand by his side. "Will you please be more specific?"

"Fine. We started out, from London, weeks ago." I stopped speaking long enough to retie the strap of my travel bonnet as I had done on that day when I left my home. Or at least I tied what was left of the strap as flames had charred the edges. "Mr. Willicks and I traveled through cities, towns, farms, and in-betweens until we reached

Liverpool. There, he dismissed our driver and we boarded a ship, more of a boat, really, up the frigid waters to Scotland and a small town with a color in the name. I cannot be more specific. Mr. Willicks hired another carriage, horse, and driver to take us to our final destination. Any questions, so far?"

"A couple, but I'll wait. Go on."

"Fine." I cleared my throat and realized how dry my mouth had become. "We were moving along at a nice pace with no impediments aside from the atrocious grounds here in Scotland when the carriage broke loose, flipped over and smashed into pieces."

"That's it?"

"What else could I possibly add?"

We stared in silence at one another, although for what reason I could not say.

"Where is your chaperone? Where is the driver?" Calum asked. Perfectly good questions and important information I should have included. I would not admit it, of course.

"I do not know why you think it is relevant," I lied, "but I shall answer you anyway. I have no idea where the driver is, however, Mr. Willicks must be out in search of assistance."

"Right. Your chaperone? You spoke to him after the accident?" he asked.

"Well, no," I admitted. "He was gone when I came to. But he is a superb chaperone and I assume he will return for me. It is his duty to do so."

"What does he look like?"

Strange question, I thought, but kept that to myself. Perhaps Calum would go looking for Mr. Willicks. "He is of average height, dark hair, dark eyes, long, dark cloak with a dark hat."

"Was he carrying a black satchel and a cane with a silver topper?"

"How did you know?" I asked. "Did you see him? Did he say he was going to contact my uncle or when he will be able to get me to my destination?"

"I saw him up the tree line from here. I called out to him to see if he needed assistance. He ran in the opposite direction."

"You must have startled him. He cannot be used to seeing young men in kilts wandering the forest. I am certain he will be back for me with proper care and proper passage."

"Right," Calum said but I did not like his tone, "about that proper passage. You don't know your destination. Do you know why you were going there?"

"Of course, I do!"

"You didn't know where you were or where you were going. How was I to know you knew anything about your journey? Come on, then."

I wrung my hands together and fought hard not to bite my bottom lip. I somewhat succeeded. There was no one else to help me. I had to tell him something, but not everything.

"My uncle sent me to deliver a message."

"A message?"

"Yes, a message. A message of upmost importance." Was that a difficult concept for a young Scottish man to understand?

"To who?"

Resisting the urge to correct his grammar, I answered. "To a Mr. Kingsnot Silver."

"Mr. Kingsnot Silver."

"Why must you keep repeating me? Are you hard of hearing?"

Calum pressed both hands on the sides of his head by the outsides of his eyes. He made little circles with his fingers, squeezing his eyelids shut. Poor thing needed a healer.

"Okay. You were on a journey, you don't know where, to deliver a message from your uncle in London to a Mr. Kingsnot Silver somewhere in Scotland. Is that right?"

"That is correct."

Calum looked up at the sun and muttered. He appeared to be doing some sort of negotiating with himself.

"Right. We need to get moving."

"Moving? To where? How?"

"Away from here. As fast as possible. Unless you wanted to be here after the sun sets, the tide changes and birds come for the fish while larger animals scavenge the horse meat. Any more questions?"

I needed time to think. My stomach tightened as we spoke. Could I trust this strange young man who was older than me by maybe a year or two and traveled the woods alone? Waiting at the wreck site with the elements closing in would be putting myself in grave danger. Was it any safer to go off into the wilderness with this Scot?

"I need my trunk."

"No. The trunk stays."

"Absolutely not!" I stated. "That trunk belonged to my mother. Besides, how will I carry everything?"

"Everything stays. We can only bring things we can trade for food or shelter."

"Please say 'lodging' not food and shelter like we are barbarians."

"Mercy, we must move now! The coming animals do not care about your finery, only about what they can eat!"

Not many people used my name. My uncle called me "child" and Mr. Willicks referred to me as "his charge" to other people. It was odd hearing my name out loud. Shrugging away the discomfort, I laid my lightweight shawl on the ground, dropped the clothes I could find – an apron, another shift, a lace kerchief, and one other skirt on top. Loud screeching, shrieking sounds came from a distance but I could not identify what was making them. I fought to tie the ends of the shawl together.

Calum stood, his mouth in a tight line, shifting his eyes between me and the edge of the woods. Apparently, Scottish men did not assist young ladies as they struggled. I shifted the strap of my satchel across my body, grabbed the bundle by the tied section, and flung it over my shoulder.

"You expect me to carry it for you?"

"I am perfectly capable." Although it did ease my fears a bit that he was gentleman enough to ask, even if it was not a sincere offer.

"I give you less than a day."

I tried to figure out what he meant when another thought came to me.

"How do I know you will not hurt or rob me?" I asked him. "Why should I trust you?"

He looked at me and without changing his expression said, "I'm the only one here."

The sky darkened as a huge group of birds appeared and headed right for us. The clattering noises they made were deafening. Calum had been right. The animals had come for the horse meat and whatever else they could find.

"What about Mr. Willicks?" I asked, although, in my heart I knew the answer.

"Don't worry about him," Calum said. "He's not coming back."

Chapter Three

W e ran. I was comforted to see that a few blue and orange butterflies flew along our path. Calum took off toward the tall
trees in the opposite direction from the horde of birds. While the
individual birds were not terribly large, together they made horrible
cackling sounds. I did not wait to see how sharp their talons were.
I followed my escort as fast as I could with my bundle and satchel
slowing my movements. We had not progressed a full ten yards in the
woods before I tripped and fell.

"Calum!" I yelled. He looked back then returned to help me to my
feet. He grabbed my bundle then zig-zagged through the leafy vines of
ground cover and around the tree trunks at an alarming rate of speed.
I traced his path as best I could, afraid I would again trip on a vine or
smack face-first into one of the gnarled tree trunks.

We ran so far and so fast that I developed a dizziness and a painful
cramp on my left side. Add to that the ever-present pain in my club
foot and our escape went from difficult to arduous. In my mind, I
begged Calum to slow down but could not gather enough breath for
a whimper, much less a sentence. My legs wobbled and I stumbled,
barely catching myself. In front of me, Calum reached the peak of a
hillock and disappeared. Had he abandoned me? The heartless savage! I crested the hillock and felt a hand grab my ankle. I screamed as
Calum pulled me backward to the ground.

"Quiet!" Calum ordered me in a harsh whisper.

"Will the birds not follow us?"

Calum clasped his hand on my mouth. What did he think he was
doing? I twisted, trying to free my face from the grip of his grime-en-
crusted hand. He gripped harder. Outrage and fear fought for control

of my actions. Fear won and I stayed still and soundless. Calum eased his grip on my mouth. Nasty animal smells lingered on his fingers and brought to mind all manner of disgusting things he had been in contact with before he touched my face. Gross.

We stayed like a bizarre statue, Calum on his back and my back on his belly, for what felt like hours. While struggling to keep my panting quiet, I strained to hear any sounds from the birds. How long did Calum plan to have us lie in the muck? When he did release me, he held his finger to his lips to indicate I should stay silent. As if I were not already. He lifted himself high enough to peek over the hillock.

He sighed and fell back down next to me.

"They're not following," he said. "To answer your question, yes they could have come after us but why chase dinner if one is sitting in front of you?"

I tried to push away pangs of guilt, sadness, and disgust but the grotesque images in my head of the winged beasts ripping apart that beautiful horse would not budge.

"We didn't have a choice but to hide. You were about to trip again or drop from exhaustion."

"I kept up!" How dare he think of me as the reason we had to lie in the mud? He had been the one to stop and pull me to the ground.

"Right. Before we get on, did you have jewelry, good pottery, or anything else we should go back for?"

"I am not in the habit of traveling with good pottery."

"Some travelers keep strange things with them."

I did not want to know how Calum had come to have knowledge of what travelers carry.

"Right. Let's get moving." He picked up the bundle, turned his back to me and started walking. "We have a long way to go. On foot."

Calum had no idea how painful those last two words were for me. The defect that made my foot turn inward would make this a painful journey. It was not the time to tell him. In fact, I hoped to never tell him at all.

"Where are you taking me?"

"To Red Rob."

"What is a Red Rob?"

"He is a who, not a what. Red Rob MacGregor. He is the leader of our clan and may know something about this Mr. Silver. If not, at least he will counsel you on what to do next."

"How would he know Mr. Kingsnot Silver?"

"Do you have any better ideas?" He paused and waited for a response. I had none.

"Right." Calum started moving again.

"I can carry my bundle," I said.

"Aye, and you will. Nae, not until I know you can walk without tripping."

If he wanted to act superior by carrying my clothes, fine by me. I wiped my face with a corner of my sleeve. It did not relieve the feeling of sweat, slime, and grit that caked my skin. My bonnet had fallen off my head during our escape and my hair was a tangled mess. I had been with Calum for near an hour and already looked and smelled like a savage.

Calum had us moving at a quick pace despite my slight limp. Rushing along in silence was boring and yet it required my constant attention. I grew tired of dodging the thorns and sharp-edged plant life encroaching on our path. Even though Calum pulled them aside for me, they still managed to snag on my clothes and slice at my arms and legs. When riding in the carriage, the scenery had moved about me instead of me moving about it. At least as a passenger, my mind could wander to more pleasant things. I would think of the crackle and pop of embers burning in the big fireplace at my uncle's in London. Life was simple and regimented. There were trips to the market, lessons to learn, tapestries to weave, and simple chores to keep.

"Mind your step here," Calum instructed. There were tree roots twice the width of my arm running along the ground; tripping over them would not be difficult.

"How, uh-hum, how much longer until we get there?" I asked. It had been so long since I had spoken, I needed to clear my throat. I ached for water.

"A day or two. Depending on how slow you walk."

I stopped. Calum stood in front of me holding back the branch of a thorny bush, waiting for me to pass. The moon lit his face and I could see he had not spoken in jest. He was serious.

"Days? Did you say one to two days?"

"Aye. Longer if you don't keep moving."

"Are we not headed to an inn or a friend for lodging?"

"An inn? Out here? No. There is no inn. We will make camp when and where we can until we meet up with the clan."

"You expect me to traipse through the wilderness for days? Carrying that huge bundle?"

"I am lugging the huge bundle at the moment, the bundle I told you to leave behind. To be clear, we will still be in what you call 'the wilderness' when we arrive. There will be no inns, houses, castles, crannogs, bothies, or a baile of any kind. We will be joining other people. There is safety in being with others."

Dangers, too. I was not familiar with the "others" to whom Calum had referred. Were they all like him? Were they more polite? Or more savage? It did not matter. I had no choice but to follow Calum and hope for the best.

"We can stop to rest in an hour or so if you're tired," Calum said.

"That would be lovely, thank you." I needed to sit, catch my breath, and think about what to do next. I had to find a way to accomplish my task. Tasks, really.

My uncle was not a warm man, but not unkind either. Being a merchant, he was able to be sure I had food, clothing, and lessons, but we did not talk about anything beyond the weather and other polite conversation. He did not ask me how I felt about being a lifelong orphan, nor did he tell me anything about my parents. At times, I would indulge in foolish, childish dreams of what it would have been like if mother and father had not been killed by a runaway horse when I was a baby. Usually, I imagined my father a tall, dashing statesmen. My mother would sit beside him and gently admonish him for his brashness. She was always beautiful, always a lady and always, always, always smiling at me.

Perhaps if my uncle had trusted me more, I would not be left dependent on the help of a Highland savage. How would I figure out a way to accomplish my task and deliver the message? Moreover, I ached to complete the part of my mission I had left out when explaining my situation to Calum. I wanted answers about my family.

My only choice was to trust Calum.

Chapter Four

My stomach rumbled and I wondered if we would be able to find something to eat soon. What I really craved was water to ease my scratchy throat. The only words spoken between us were Calum telling me to "mind your step" and me thanking him. I did not want to thank him, as his constant assistance made me seem like a dim child, but it is what one does in polite society.

Calum continued to rub his head so I searched along the ground for feverfew as we trekked through the woods. A bit of the plant would soon ease his headache, if not make it disappear completely. In truth, anything on our stomachs, even a few small plants, would help us both have clearer heads. Water would help as well.

We walked a little farther before I noticed a butterfly with soft blue wings flutter through a few beams of morning light peeking through tree branches. The light landed on a small crop of clover and feverfew. I ran toward it. Calum launched his cloak toward me and it landed on my head.

"What are you doing?" I demanded, waving my arms as I tried to free myself from the sea of cloth. How big was his cloak? I found myself desperate to breathe fresh air again.

"You were running. I assumed there was danger nearby." He, to my further annoyance, deftly removed the cloak from my head.

"And drowning me in your cloak would help?" I attempted to smooth my hair. It was useless, of course. The tight, neat bun that I had pained to fix before donning my journey bonnet was long gone.

"I was giving you the only cover I had, not knowing whatever it was you were running from. It was a gut reaction. Where's the threat?"

"I was running to something, not from it," I told him then pointed to the feverfew.

"You want to pick daisies?"

"Eat them," I corrected. "They are feverfew, which are excellent for easing headaches."

"I thought you said you were from London."

"I am. What does that have to do with our present conversation?"

"How do you know about plants and how to use them?"

"Do you not think we have healers in London? How do you imagine we deal with our ailments?"

"Where do you get plants in the city?"

"There are many parks and fields throughout our grand city. Markets are full of fresh herbs for foods, scent sachets, and of course, healing. Vendors come from both inside the city and the nearby countryside. You see, I am not such a city mouse that I do not appreciate country things."

"You think me a country mouse, afraid of the perils of the city?"

"You seem to think it is full of clogged roads and sickly creatures." I paused for a heartbeat, trying to decide whether or not to say what I was thinking. "I am surprised you know the fables."

"You think I am dumb to everything but the Highlands?"

"No." Well, sort of. "I am merely surprised you knew of Aesop and his tales. They are quite ancient."

"The seannachie told them along with the clan history and any other story that is important to being a MacDonald."

"Is that your clan, the MacDonalds?"

"It was."

That seemed an odd response and Calum quickened his step after he gave it. I took that as an indication he felt our conversation had ended. Any more questions I had would have to wait. As well as getting Calum to try the feverfew.

We had walked through the night. The weather was not too warm and the trees shielded us from the direct sun but my body still produced slick sweat. The need to quench my thirst became all I could think about, not even my hunger pangs distracted me for long. I tried to soothe myself by observing my environment. The trees were tall but thin. Once in a while, one would be leaning on its neighbor, held up by the other's roots. It occurred to me they looked like a family. Or at least how I imagined a family would be.

The density of the trees was growing thinner and thinner and I hoped we were getting to the edge of the forest and into a village of some sort, perhaps built along the side of a fresh water river. A crow or raven or some such bird made a noise and I looked up through the trees to the right. My eyes did not find the calling bird in the distance but found something much better. Smoke.

"Do you see it?" I asked keeping my eyes fixed as if losing sight of it would make it disappear.

Calum looked up at me, then followed my line of sight to the smoke, rising calm and beautiful as if it happened all the time. That kind of rising smoke could mean only one thing. Chimney smoke. Somewhere up there was a house where people lived.

"Do you think they are friendly?" I asked.

"There's one way to find out," Calum replied and continued picking our way through the woods. "When we get there, let me talk. Your accent will give you away."

"Give me away?" I asked. "As what?" I was insulted by his suggestion, although I could not say why.

"As English. Not Scottish."

"We are all ruled by the same king."

Calum made a quiet snorting noise. "In this part of Scotland, that does not matter. The English are not looked upon as countrymen."

The English not countrymen with Scots? Fine with me.

It took more than a quarter hour or so to get close enough to see the source of the smoke. Never had I been so happy to see a chimney.

The stone structure sat on the end of a small, somewhat-wobbly stone house which had a thatched roof, a single tiny window and a large door. A smaller building with no chimney or window sat next to it. Large trees surrounded the two buildings giving them the look of being quite guarded.

"Wait here," Calum said.

I was growing weary of being ordered around by Calum. What made him think he knew best in every situation? I ignored his instruction and followed close behind as he approached the house.

"Right," he said when he noticed me.

I did not speak a response. I shrugged instead.

When we were less than a yard from the door which I could now see was two sizes too large for the small house, Calum called out to see if anyone was home. There was no answer.

"It seems there is no one here. The smaller building probably holds some hay for a horse or cattle. We can try to get some sleep here or we can keep going."

I leaned back from Calum. "Are you asking me what we should do?"

"I am asking if you are okay with breaking into the barn and sleeping in hay."

Oh. That was a good question. One week ago, I would never have considered bedding down on hay in a barn like a common beast. On this day, I was grateful for it.

Chapter Five

A loud crack came from the distance. Was it the owner of the house coming back? Or was it a large animal in search of food? Which would be preferable?

"Should we run?" I asked. "This is not exactly a place that welcomes strangers."

"Highlanders are gracious hosts, even when the guests are unexpected."

That was yet to be determined in my view.

"Remember, let me talk to them. Your proper English and your accent will make people concerned the King's men are nearby. Do you want that?"

Apparently not. His words began to sink into my mind. "I cannot speak at all?"

"Try to keep your voice low. Mumble, if you can but don't be rude."

"How can I both mumble and not be rude?"

"Give it a try."

Calum headed out to meet whom he assumed would be warm Highland hosts. I hung back in order to check the security and concealment of my pockets. Satisfied that no one would be able to see them, I stood closer to, but behind Calum so I could hear everything but not be seen straight away.

A man of substantial size came into view. His hair was the color of tree bark and grew past his shoulders. His mustache and beard were nothing more than stubble. He was not dressed in a Highland kilt but in pants made of a tartan pattern. His horse looked sad and perhaps ill. He smelled that way, too.

Both Calum's and the homeowner's voices were calm and sociable but a bit cautious. Calum explained we were on a journey and had come upon his place quite by accident. He turned toward me as in invitation to come closer and join them.

The moment I stepped forward, the expression on the homeowner's face went from pleasant to sour. The horse snorted. What had I done? I had yet to open my mouth.

I did not curtsy or extend my hand. I nodded in his general direction. After getting a better look, he reminded me of a bear from my childhood lessons. Of course, I had only seen drawings of bears but his size and gruffness reminded me of them.

"Aye, sir." Calum held his hand in the air as if to get Bear Man's attention before he could turn and leave us. "Could we do a chore in exchange perhaps for a bit of meat?"

"Chores, eh?" the man grunted. He scratched his hand along the growth on his chin. "I could use someone to chop wood. My back does not want to do the work at times." Bear Man's expression became suspicious when his glance shifted from Calum to me. The look in his eyes made me fearful. Did he know I was not Scottish? That was not possible. Right?

"Aye, sir. I'd be proud to split some logs for you. I'll make quick work of it, too."

"Fine, fine. The pile is around back. Try not to make a mess of things." He left us where we stood and walked to his front door, one hand leading his horse, the other rubbing his own back.

"Good. With a wee bit of work, we will have something in our stomachs," Calum said.

"He did not say he would feed us. All he said was that you could chop some wood."

"He is a Highlander. He will give us what he can spare. Let's get to work."

I was not so sure this Highland hospitality would extend to me but

Calum seemed upbeat. We walked around to the back of the house. Large logs were strewn about in a misshapen pile along the edge of the trees. Spider webs and rodent nests dotted the log heap. Nearby sat a stump with an axe swung into it but Bear Man had not chopped wood for quite some time. Calum could not chop enough to get him through the next winter, but he would be warm tonight. Would we?

Calum wasted no time pulling the axe from its resting place and placing the first log so one of the small sides faced up. Leaning the axe handle on one of his legs, he closed his eyes and rubbed both sides of his head. I searched the ground for feverfew and found some nearby.

"Here," I offered. "Have some."

"Some what? Weeds?"

"No. Weeds would do nothing for you. These are feverfew."

"They look like daisies."

"Fine, then they are daisies. Now eat them."

"Right. Em, no thanks."

"They will help your headache and make this chore go quicker. Besides, you have nothing on your stomach and feverfew, or daisies, are better than nothing."

He seemed to accept this as truth and took a few from my hand. I expected him to look them over and ask more questions, delaying the inevitable but to my surprise, he chomped down on the heads of the flowers and kept chewing and swallowing until they were all gone.

"Now what?"

"Nothing. You wait for them to work. You should feel better soon."

Calum shrugged, wiped plant debris on his shirt and picked up the axe.

"There must be water nearby," I said. "In which direction do you suppose I should look?"

"Fill this for me." He pulled out a small canteen from the folds of his cloak and handed it to me. It was thin, short, and rectangular.

I nodded. Calum pointed in the direction of the water and I headed out with a quicker step than I had had all day. I was so thirsty my lips were cracking but as I headed to the water, quenching the most intense thirst I had ever experienced was not my main goal. I had no idea why the man of the house disliked me but I thought I knew a way to change his sour opinion.

Chapter Six

I could hear the *shushshushshush* of the stream before I could see the water rush past high grasses on the banks. Bird calls pierced the air every few seconds as they talked amongst themselves. I wondered if they were warning each other of my presence. The tiny creatures of the wetland were buzzing and clicking and squeaking as they went about their daily tasks. I followed the buzzes and clicks as bees and butterflies were likely to be busy around the plants I needed.

The silver-white underside of a common blue butterfly stood out from the green leaves and brought my eyes to the comfrey, a lovely flower with its dark violet petals hanging down in pretty fluted shapes. I longed to drink from the stream but the flowered herbs needed to be harvested before I could tend to my own needs. As I gathered the deepest colored plants, I wondered how this trek was going to help me get to Mr. Kingsnot Silver. Since I lacked both the money and time to return to London or even post a letter to my uncle, I had to rely on Calum to continue to help me.

Snap!

I paused for a moment to be sure I had heard it.

Snap!

Something behind me was stepping on twigs. If it was large enough to snap twigs, it was big enough to do me harm. I had two options, to run and hope I was faster or turn and face my aggressor. Since I did not know where I was or where I would go, I chose to stay. I stood with purpose and spun around to see my foe.

"What're yer lookin for?" Bear Man asked. Without his horse he seemed somehow larger. The fear and uncertainty that had filled me moments prior began to ebb but not disappear. I opened my mouth to speak and then remembered Calum's warning about how a Highlander would not be happy to hear a Londoner's accent. Instead of a proper sentence, I held out my bouquet of comfrey.

"Flowers, huh?" he said. "Lassies do like flowers. Especially lassies who dress like you. What are those, bluebells? There are a funny color if they are."

"No, sir," I said in my best efforts to speak as a mumbling Scottish lassie. "For your back."

"Did you say my back?"

I nodded up and down like an excited fool. This was a terrible way to communicate.

He did not reply immediately. Perhaps he paused to consider my sanity. While I awaited a response, I noticed he was carrying something metal in his hands. He saw me looking at it.

"It's a canteen," he held out the metal container. It was larger and rounder but much more scarred with age and use than the one Calum handed me. "I saw you going toward my water and figured you wanted a drink." I reached toward him to take the dirty canteen. It was warped and dented but sturdy enough to hold water. I wanted to explain that we had a canteen but did not know how without sounding too English. "Be sure to take some to the lad. He'll be thirsty when he's done." Without another word he headed back to the house. Any attempt to call out to him while mumbling to hide my accent would certainly be futile so I stood there, comfrey still in my hand.

I was thrilled to have both Calum's newer canteen and the Bear Man's hoary one. Clearly the man had owned this canteen for many years. Creaks and squeaks emanated from the cap as I unscrewed it. I dipped the container in the stream. Cool water rushing over my hand sent shivers up my arms and down my back. It felt glorious. I could not recall the last time I had felt fresh water. I pulled the canteen out of the water and drank from it. The clean cool water shocked my dry lips and mouth in a magnificent manner. The water rushed down my throat and trickled through my body to my belly. I nearly fainted with relief.

Guilt that I had refreshed myself while Calum performed his chores spurred me to get moving. I refilled the canteen one more time, filled Calum's, gathered up the comfrey for Bear Man, and headed back to the house. Even though he annoyed me nearly all the time and had a negative comment about everything I said, Calum was going out of his way to help me. But why? He could have left me where I was and continued on to wherever he had been headed. Where had he been headed? Had he told me? Did I ask?

"How much more are you going to do?" I asked when I was close enough for him to hear me. He took one more swing before he looked at me.

"Not much. More weeds to snack on?" he asked, leaning closer to the comfrey in my hands.

"No, never eat these. They are fatal if eaten."

"Then why did you bring them to me?" he asked, pulling back.

"These are for our host. This is for you." I handed him the filled canteens. He grabbed them both and started drinking in one motion. The gurgling sounds were rude but forgivable under the circumstances of extreme thirst. When he had emptied both canteens, he licked his lips to ensure he had captured every last drop.

"Where'd you get the old canteen?" he asked.

I nodded my head in the direction of the house. "He came to the stream to give it to me."

"So you decided to poison him?" He closed one eye, looked inside the larger canteen with the other as if he expected to find more water hidden there.

"What?"

"You said those weeds were fatal and for our host. The logical conclusion is that you plan to poison him."

"No, of course not!"

Considering he thought I was going to murder someone, Calum seemed calm. Too calm. He was teasing me!

"Not funny, Calum." I gave him my best look of displeasure but Calum grinned in response.

"What are they for, then? If not to poison anyone."

"These are comfrey. A quick compress will ease the ache in his back."

Before Calum could respond, Bear Man reappeared next me. Instead of a compress, I should make him a collar with a bell.

"Laddie! That is enough to keep me warm for months. I thank you."

"Thank you, sir. We have one more chore before we go. Mercy here wants to make you a compress for your back. She thinks it may ease your ache."

I did not *think* it would. I *knew* it would but kept quiet.

"Are you a healer, then, or a witch?" Bear Man asked.

The question was so plainly stated I was unsure how to respond. Calum jumped in before I could catch my breath.

"A healer, sir," he said. "She gave me daisies that quieted my headache. But she insists that eating these weeds would be deadly so a compress is needed instead. Do you have any water in your kettle?"

"Aye, yeah." Bear Man said. He turned to enter the house.

Calum and I followed, passing the horse who stood by the door. The house was more of a shed made of rocks stuck together with mud and straw and grass. It was not expertly made, leaving open slivers where air, wind and weather could enter the living space. What mattered most was that it was, if only technically, indoors. Lucky for us, the weather was calm.

Chapter Seven

A loud clap of thunder made me jump. Within seconds, fat rain-drops dropped from the sky as if from buckets. So much for calm weather.

"Garry!" Bear Man shouted. "He cannae stand thunder! He'll bolt if not tied!"

Terrific. Calum and I exchanged a glance. We headed outside and sure enough the horse, apparently named Garry, was shaking his head, stepping back and forth. He reared back on his hind legs and whinnied at the sky. After he landed on his forelegs, I held out my hand, not as if to bring him a treat, but to show him I meant no harm. Garry backed up at first but I kept moving toward him with slow, easy movements. Soon I had my hand on his nose and pet him gently while Calum grabbed his reins. The three of us walked to the barn and settled Garry in his stall.

Calum grabbed my bundle, which we had left outside the barn, on our way back to the house. We were both dripping wet messes.

"That was incredible, wee lassie!" Bear Man said when we re-turned. "I have never seen anyone control Garry like that. I am glad you already told me you are a healer and not a witch or I would have to suspect witchcraft! Let's try that press-thing there you said, with the pretty flowers."

I kept my eyes and hands busy, first braiding the comfrey stems to-gether then fussing with the cloth and boiling water our host provided for the compress. I did not want to meet Calum's gaze any sooner than I had to after our host had mentioned witchcraft twice in less than an hour. Once the comfrey was properly wrapped in cloth and laid in a shallow wooden bowl, I poured the piping hot kettle water over it. As quick as possible, I grabbed the compress out of the bowl and tossed it hand to hand until it was cool enough to hold without wincing but still warm enough to do our host some good.

I motioned to Bear Man to turn his back to me so I could apply the compress. He complied and I placed the warm compress to the spot on his back he had been rubbing. He jumped a bit, startled by the heat.

"Yow! That's hot!"

"Sorry," I mumbled. I wanted to explain that the heat helped to release the herb into his body and the hotter the better but I did not want to upset Calum by speaking. The man reached back and held the compress himself.

"I think it may be helping already," he said.

I smiled and nodded even though there was no way he could feel the effects of the herb yet. The heat gave him instant relief.

"Those purple bluebells can help my back, eh?" He spoke out loud but did not seem to be expecting an answer.

"Sounds like the rain stopped," Calum said. "Looks like it's time to get moving."

"Weather is as fickle as a young lassie in spring," Bear Man said to no one in particular. "I thank you for your help." He got out of his chair, still holding his compress on his back, and shuffled across the small space to a wooden box turned sideways for storage. He reached inside and pulled something out of a small package. "Smoked hare. It will keep your stomachs from being totally empty for a while."

"Thank you," Calum said with a big smile. "This is too much for our small chores."

What was it with Calum? Always trying to get us to do more work! The amount of wood he chopped would last the man for months. Calum had asked for meat, why was he questioning it when we got it?

"Nae, you did much more than that," Bear Man said. "You took care of Garry and this heated flower pack is really helping my back. Take the canteen, too."

"No, sir," Calum said as he tucked the meat into his waist pack. "We cannae take that from you. Mine will serve for the two of us."

"Pish!" he replied. "That's my old one. I have another." He reached into another storage box and pulled out some baked goods partially covered with dirt. "Here you go. These will get you started, anyway."

Calum took what Bear Man offered and gave me what appeared to be the cleaner portion of it. Without bothering to investigate further, we both bit into the offerings. It was some sort of roll. Delicious!

"Now, on your way," the man said. "You'll want to be moving on before the sun sets."

Chapter Eight

We headed straight to the water to drink deep from the stream. Between the two of us, we probably filled each canteen half a dozen times. Then, we feasted on morsels of actual hare meat. The rolls and smoked hare did not fill my stomach but what little I ate helped lessen the pangs and made my legs feel less wonky.

"Those daisies did a fine job on my headache."

"Feverfew. You should learn to recognize it for when you need it in the future."

"Aye, true. Let's go. We need to put a few miles behind us before we stop again."

With some sort of food in my stomach, thirst quenched for the moment and a clue as to where our next food and water would come from, my mind was able to turn to thoughts of a more productive sort. Namely, getting to Mr. Silver, wherever he was.

Calum led the way, as was proper for the situation, and pointed out the obvious perils in our path, which was not.

"Why do you assume I cannot do things for myself?" I asked.

"What? What do you mean?"

"You lead me around thorn bushes, you shelter me with your cloak, and you give me the best of the stale rolls. You know, I can do for myself."

Calum chortled. He actually chortled. So certain was he of my ineptitude that he laughed at the suggestion of my capabilities.

"You would not be alive if I had not found you and taken care of you!"

"How dare you!" I said with a snarl.

"I dare because it's the truth! You were a tattered city rat when I came upon you. If I hadn't helped you, who knows what would have happened."

"I would have taken care of myself! I am not incompetent. I would not have succumbed to some horrible disaster. If you would bother to notice, I am still tattered."

"You are city born and city lived. There is no way you could survive in the wilds of the countryside. Your long skirts would get caught on the first thistle and you would stand there and starve to death before you figured out how to untangle yourself."

"Not true! You are nothing but a country mouse, scared and squeaky. You would not last a single day in the market place. You would pay two woolen shirts for a small piece of foul cheese!"

"Is that what you think? This is not a park for strolling or a marketplace with proper manners and civility. Outlaws, clan scouts, and plain criminals lurk behind every tree. Anyone else would have robbed you and left you for dead. Like your pretentious chaperone did."

"Comment oses-tu! How dare you! I may speak with a different accent and have a larger vocabulary but that does not mean that you are better than me at anything."

"Right, if you are so good at living out here on your own, do it!"

With that, Calum dropped my bundle, turned on his heel and headed off in the opposite direction than where we had been walking. What did he think he was doing?

"Are you leaving me here?"

"You'll be fine," he called over his shoulder. "You said so yourself. In two languages."

"And if there are outlaws and unsavory men skulking about out here?" I yelled to him. "Would you leave me here to their wiles?"

"You can handle it, remember? You don't need a squeaky country mouse to help you."

"Fine!" I threw my hands in the air to show I did not care what he did.

"Right!" he yelled back.

"I'll be fine!"

"Good!"

I stood still, watching Calum blend into the trees and underbrush. My hands dampened with sweat and my heart raced. I felt as if my head would fly off from anger. How dare he think I could not take care of myself, no matter the circumstances? Had he not seen me handle the spooked horse? Had I not gotten rid of his headache and the Bear Man's back ache? How dare he think I needed anyone to help me!

I squinted, trying to catch the last glimpses of Calum's head as it disappeared. My heart slowed a beat.

How dare he leave me alone.

Well, fine. If he was too much of a savage to help me, then I would have to help myself. I picked up my bundle and started out in the direction we had been walking before Calum started yelling. I stopped after a few steps. Was that the way we were headed or the direction Calum went when he abandoned me? What did it matter now, anyway? We had been on our way to Calum's clan for help. Even if I could find them, which was highly unlikely, they would not help me now.

Here I was, back in the same position as before. Lost. Directionless. Maybe a tiny bit scared. With no way to complete my mission.

Chapter Nine

S tanding alone in the woods without a clue as to which direction to head, I could hear my heart beating and the loud exhale of my breath. Why had Calum bothered to stop and pretend to help me, only to leave me lost in another part of the same woods? Was it entertainment for him?

No matter, now. What did matter was getting to Mr. Silver by midsummer and for that I needed help. I dropped my bundle and used it as a make-shift stool, easing the pressure on my foot. Perhaps Bear Man could offer assistance. I won him over by calming his horse and helping his backache. Getting back there required remembering from what direction we had come. It frightened me to think how quick I had become dependent on Calum, wholly accepting his word on every topic to do with our travels. I had not been tracking our path or paying any attention to our surroundings. My uncle would be aghast at what I had allowed to happen to me.

I came up with a plan to figure out which direction led back to Bear Man. With the bundle as my anchor, I would walk in a straight line in one direction, counting each step until I reached one hundred. While doing so, I would look to see if I recognized anything. At step one hundred, I would return to the bundle, then walk in another direction doing the same tasks. I would continue the pattern until I was certain which path was correct.

I lifted myself from my seat and I walked forward, counting out loud. Perhaps it was to hear something besides my heartbeat and breath and perhaps it was to frighten off any would-be attackers, but counting out loud seemed the logical thing to do. Concentrating on the trees and trying to remember if I had seen any particular one before, it struck me how similar trees look to one another. Tall, thin, bark-covered trunks with long limbs that had needled branches poking out in all directions. Or shorter, chubbier trunks with splaying leaves on sagging limbs. When the sun set, which would be much sooner than I wanted this evening, those same branches would look malicious, evil even. I shivered at the unpleasant thought.

"One hundred," I said to myself and the trees. "Okay, now turn around and go back."

I spun one-hundred-eighty degrees and began the walk back. Other noises reached my ears. Birds taking off from branches, landing on other tree limbs. The scuttle of rodents and other small creatures moving through the growth of ground-cover along the forest floor. The scratching of nails as some animals climbed the bark of trees. It was comforting that I could hear these other sounds. Perhaps it meant I was calming down which would make it easier to carry out my plan. Cooler heads are always wiser.

I had no verifiable idea which creatures lived in Scottish forests but I assumed birds, squirrels, moles, chipmunks, voles, shrews, and small feral cats as in the woods near the park at home. Possibly deer, as well. Of course, it was Scotland. There could be unicorns in these woods for all I knew.

As I recounted the possible animals in the forest and congratulated myself on my calmness, the kind face of my childhood governess, Miss Mopley, flashed in my mind. Without acquaintances my own age, I spent most of my young childhood hours with Miss Mopley. She left us when I turned seven. How I would love to see her face in person right now and have her tell me that I am a smart child and will figure a way out of this forest in order to do what I came to this odd country to do. How did this journey get so off-track?

I caught a flash of movement out of the corner of my eye. It was gone by the time I turned my head for a better look. Had I made it up? Was something there or was my mind going funny? If it was real, it was too big to be a squirrel or feral cat but too small to be a unicorn.

I stood still for a moment, quiet as could be, and listened. My mind played pictures of nefarious men creeping about the forest, looking to rob or harm me but my eyes yielded no such reality. A breeze blew the branches making a faint rustling sound and I tried my best not to die of fright on the spot.

"You are being ridiculous, Mercy," I said out loud to myself. "Thirty- seven. You were on step thirty-seven."

I continued to count and walk as straight a line as possible back to my starting position. Around step number seventy-nine, I could see my worthless bundle in the spot where I left it. Something large was sitting on top. Actually it was someone.

Calum.

Neither of us spoke or even looked at the other until I was standing toe-to-toe with him.

"You are sitting on my property," I said without my voice showing a quiver of my anger.

"Why did you count on your way back?" he asked.

"What?"

"You counted on the way back. You would know when you got to a hundred because you'd see your bundle but you kept counting, until you saw me."

"If I counted to one hundred and was not standing in front of my bundle, then I would know I had gone askew as opposed to not reaching it yet."

We were both silent again. A forest creature, a squirrel perhaps, scratched the bark as it climbed the tree behind me. The sound annoyed me.

"Why would knowing you were lost make you any less lost?"

"I would know for sure that I was lost and should retrace my steps to find the bundle." He was acting quite dense about something that no longer mattered. "Why were you spying on me in the woods?"

"I wasn't spying," Calum chided calmly. "I returned because I did not give you your share of the food."

"You need not have troubled yourself," I said. It bothered me when he used that tone. "I would have been fine."

"Right," he said, even though we both knew it was a lie. "There was also the matter of this."

He reached in the folds of his cloak and pulled out the small bag of cash he had taken from the lining of Mr. Willicks's trunk. How could I have forgotten about the money? It was possibly the one thing that could help me.

"I could've walked off with it," Calum said. "In fact, I did. Do you even know how much is in here?"

I shook my head and shifted my eyes to the ground, feeling ashamed that I could be so careless. Calum was right to lecture me this time, although, it did not make me any less irritated with him. Well, maybe a little.

"Right, because you never asked. You let me take it and did not ask to carry it or count it. You are lucky I take Highland honor seriously."

I had reached my point of absorbing his lecture so I straightened my back and lifted my chin to meet his gaze.

"Well then, how much is in it?"

"Hopefully enough to get you where you need to go, wherever that is." He held it out for me to take.

"I can take care of myself, you know," I said without taking the money, "but it would be faster and easier if you helped me."

"Take the money."

"I mean, I can find my way but you know these woods and whatever lays beyond them. You can navigate me through with little effort." A little flattery never hurts when you need a favor.

"Take the money."

I could take the money and try to venture through the wilderness hoping to solve an unsolvable riddle and survive these treacherous conditions, all in time to deliver the message. Or I could do whatever it took to get Calum to help me. I felt as if I had no true choice but that did not make what I had to do next any easier.

"Is it honorable for a Highlander to abandon a young lady in need who has asked for his help?"

Calum dropped the arm that still held Mr. Willicks's sack of cash. He let out a deep sigh and from the look on his face it appeared his headache was returning.

"I did not hear you ask for my help."

"I said your assistance would make the trip faster and easier."

"A statement of fact. Not a request."

"You want me to formally request your assistance before you will help me?"

"Before I will consider helping you." Calum crossed his arms and leaned back on my bundle as if to indicate that he could wait a long time.

I did not think this humiliation was necessary. I had known Calum a short while but knew he would help me. If he wanted me to ask nicely, so be it.

"Fine. Calum, sir, I do hereby formally request the honor of your indispensable skills needed to complete my task. Can you find it in your heart to acquiesce and render assistance?"

Calum waited a beat, then stood up.

"Yes, but under one condition. Tell me the truth about why you're in Scotland."

Chapter Ten

"The truth? I told you the truth. Besides, your one condition was for me to ask for your help, remember?"

"Right, this is a second condition. You've said vague statements about a mission that has something to do with a man with the oddest name I have ever heard. Frankly, Mercy, you sound like a lass playing games."

Playing? How could he accuse me of being frivolous? I was being vague, that was true and rather astute of him but I could not tell him the whole truth.

"Well?"

Without Calum's contacts and knowledge of the area, I would never get where I needed to be by midsummer and all I had done would be for nothing. Plus, I would never get the answers I needed about from where I came and whom my family truly was.

"Fine." I took a turn sitting on my bundle. After a big breath to ease my nerves, I filled Calum in on the details. "I have been training for this mission for as long as I can remember. My uncle hired the best tapestry tutors, herbalists, and historical scholars to prepare me. My parents were the ones who were supposed to train me but their deaths put an end to that."

Calum's stern expression softened the slightest when I mentioned my orphaned status.

"The purpose of my mission is to reconnect the parties of the Auld Alliance."

Calum did not immediately respond. Perhaps stunned at what I had revealed.

"But, you're English," Calum said. "The Auld Alliance bound France and Scotland together for extra protection against England, back before the Union of the Crowns when Scotland had her own king."

"True, I was raised in London but born in France."

"Right." Calum paused before continuing. "Emm, isn't the Auld Alliance, you know, gone?" he asked.

"Every twelve years, at midsummer, one Scottish lass and one French maiden travel to the other country and show the friendship is intact. Each will deliver the same message and perform the same task as every messenger before her. I am the French girl whose life's purpose is to go to Scotland and prove the French still care about the Alliance."

"What happens if you don't make it on time?" Calum asked. He had begun pacing a small route in front of me. He was really pushing the boundaries of my patience with all these questions. I had no choice but to answer them because I needed Calum's help but I frowned at him before responding.

"I do not know. It is my great misfortune that my parents were unable to prepare me. My uncle got me the basics of what I need but there are many things I do not understand."

"So it might be no big deal if you do not get there until the next day?" he asked.

"Or it may mean the end to the world's oldest, longest, and strongest Alliance."

Calum studied me before speaking again.

"Do you believe that? Is that why you are so set on getting there on time?"

I had no idea what would happen to the Alliance if I did not get to the meet up on time. Nor did I know what would happen to the world if the Alliance faltered. There was one other reason I needed to arrive on time. It could be the only chance I had to learn about my family and the people who came before me. Did I want Calum to know that reason?

"I do not know," I said. "What I do know is that my parents believed it was important enough that they made sure my uncle knew to pre-pare me in case they could not. I cannot disappoint them."

Calum rubbed his chin instead of the sides of his head. Then he let out a long sigh and held out his hand to help me to my feet.

"We better get moving," he said.

"I do not think anyone else needs to know the details of my mission."

Calum nodded. "Agreed. It's best we keep this between us. At least for now."

From the bundle, I pulled out my light-weight shawl and my extra apron and stuffed them in my satchel. I dropped the bag of cash in as Calum insisted. He said nothing as we walked away, leaving the rest of my belongings to the animals. I gave him credit for not saying the "I told you so" that hung in the air between us. Strange images flashed in my mind of forest creatures running around in my clothes. It did not make me laugh.

"Do you really think the woods are full of unsavory thieves?"

Calum shrugged. "It is possible thieves are around, but the woods are usually full of clan scouts. That's why I'm here."

"Are they about tonight?" I grasped my tattered cloak a bit tighter around my neck. "The clan scouts, I mean. I do not wish to run across them in the dark."

"No need to worry. This particular night, the clansmen are not apt to go on a mission. They will be too busy trying to impress each other with their tales of glory. Red Rob has been to Edinburgh and will re-turn tonight. He will bring great lies of astounding connections with noble men whom he will claim will get us what is rightfully ours."

With all of Calum's talk of honor, he did not speak with reverence about his leader.

"How do you know they will be lies?" I asked.

"They always are. The hard truth is, we live this way because it is how we fit in the world. Someone has to challenge the great men with their many heads of cattle. Why do they deserve all that wealth simply because something terrible never happened to them? Why do we not deserve such things just because my parents were brutally murdered on the orders of one of those great men Red Rob meets with? They don't intend to help us any more than MacGregors intend to stop rustling cattle. This is our place in the world."

Perhaps it was MacGregor's place in the world but I did not believe it was Calum's.

Chapter Eleven

We walked as the sun got lower and soon we were out of the forest and hiking across long stretches of grass. Heather and prickly bushes grew in clusters alongside large groups of rocks. In the forest, I felt as if danger surrounded me. It seemed that unknown perils lurked in limbs overhead and behind tree trunks and degenerate criminals were eager to rob me of my meager possessions. I longed to be out of the darkness and in an open field, yet now that I was, it felt less safe. There was nowhere to hide.

I busied myself with thoughts of Calum and his clan. How did a young man who revered honor, to the point that he returned with my money, wind up reporting to someone he did not respect at all?

"How did you come to meet Mr. MacGregor?" I asked.

"You don't meet Rob Roy MacGregor, he allows you in his presence." Calum's distaste for this man was palpable.

"Well, is his name Rob or Roy?"

"Rob Raudh."

"Rob Roy?"

"Raudh, not Roy. Raudh is Gaelic for red because he has red hair."

"Rob Roy means Rob Red?"

"Aye, yeah. But we, his clansmen, call him Red Rob."

"What should I call him, then?"

"You shouldn't."

We walked a while longer in uncomfortable silence. First, I was not allowed to speak in front of Bear Man because my accent and grammar would cause issue and now I could not speak to this Gaelic fellow, who was probably more of a savage than Bear Man could ever be, because I was not a member of his clan? Would I be allowed to speak above a whisper to anyone except Calum in all my time in Scotland?

"That is lunacy. Why can I not speak to him directly? I am not a child."

"That is of no matter to Red Rob. What matters is you are not of his clan."

"That is absurd. I will tell him that myself when I speak to him because I certainly plan to do so. You cannot stop me."

"Nor do I plan to stop you. I simply said you shouldn't speak to him, not that you can't. But know this: I will not be able to stop whatever comes next."

We walked on and I rolled over in my mind what Calum had said, trying to picture this man whom Calum described. The more I thought about his strange ways and aversion to strangers, the more determined I became to talk to him myself. If Calum thought MacGregor could help me find Mr. Silver, then I had to do everything possible to get that help. Calum might not push hard enough without my prompting and I was running out of time. Every sunset brought us closer to midsummer, the deadline to deliver my message.

"Wait here." Calum did not wait for a response. He held up his hand to tell me to stop and crept toward a nearby boulder.

"More orders? Really, Calum, I do not see why you think you can command me..."

Calum snapped his head back in my direction while staying in his crouch and put his forefinger to his lips in the unmistakable sign for immediate silence. The concerned look in his eyes made me comply, albeit with reluctance. I nodded to signal my intent to remain quiet.

Assured of my temporary muteness, Calum returned his attention to the boulder. There was nothing out of the ordinary about the big rock, other than the fact that it was not nearby any other rock of any size. Is that what upset Calum? Perhaps it was not the boulder itself but rather what was hiding behind it. Was it an animal searching prey?

A thief waiting to rob us, and when he found we had nothing of value, to kill us?

At that thought, I resolved to heed Calum's instructions without reserve. Calum kept his crouch, silent and still, hands at the ready. I followed his physical example and bent down as well. His ear leaned forward in a small movement aimed toward the boulder. I held my breath, not in a conscience effort to go undetected by whatever was behind that rock, but in anticipation of what would happen next. If an animal or thief did attack, would Calum be able to protect us? Would he want to protect me?

Scuffling sounds of an animal adjusting its weight and rubbing against the far side of the boulder brought my mind to sharp focus once again. My stomach tightened and a sick feeling flooded my body. I feared I would be unable to run, should Calum instruct me to. Calum's body did not move. Years of lurking in the woods and living under the reign of the Gaelic man must have taught him how to observe without being observed. It was most impressive to watch.

As soon as I thought that, his body language changed, as if to prove me wrong. He dropped his hands and stood up straight.

"Alright, you've had your fun!" he called out. "Show your faces, you scurvy lassies."

At his command, three young Scots, men, not women, about Calum's age but larger on all sides including height, came tumbling out from behind the boulder. They were dirtier and a might bit smellier than Calum. Dressed in kilts, long shirts and cloaks, even in the warm afternoon sun, they were the picture of Highland savages. They were all Scottish lads, living in the wilderness, following orders from the same man. Yet Calum truly did not look like these young men and it was more than the simple fact that the other three were obviously brothers. There was a gentleness to him the others did not possess.

I was so surprised that Calum knew them that I could not find my voice. Did they try to scare us to death for their own amusement? How was that funny?

"What is the matter with you three?" Calum asked.

"Having a bit of fun," one of them replied.

"Yeah, when we saw you, we knew we had a chance to get you to do your crouch thing," another added.

All three of them began to imitate Calum's crouch with remarkable precision and mockery. They even had stern looks on their faces, except the youngest looking one. He could not contain his smile. One of the older brothers hit the smiling one hard in the shoulder and the three of them laughed themselves silly, until one of them opened his eyes enough to see me staring at him. I tried to keep my thoughts off my face but am not sure how successful I was.

"Who's this?" the second of the older brothers asked, cocking his head in my direction as if I were a plant or a painting or something.

"Mercy," Calum said to me. "These are three of my fellow clansmen, Ailean, Girvan and Dugal."

Having been raised in London, I knew that the appropriate greeting would be to curtsy, at least a little, bow my head, smile, and say, "Lovely to make your acquaintance." Then I should find some sort of appropriate comment to make in order to continue the conversation in a friendly tone. None of those things seemed right in this particular scenario. I did my best to adjust.

"Good day, Ailean. Girvan. Dugal." I sort of nodded in their general direction. "Brothers, I presume?"

The three Scots stared at me as they blinked five or six times, then turned their gazes to Calum. At the same moment, they erupted in boisterous laughter, hitting each other repeatedly with full force blows. It was terrible to watch. This was how they expressed themselves?

"Let's get back," Calum said. "There is much to do before dark."

Chapter Twelve

Calum resumed walking in our path and at our usual pace. For several hundred yards after meeting them, Ailean, Girvan, and Dugal continued to punch and jostle each other. It seemed their only form of communication. Once in a while they would send a blow Calum's way. He would return it and keep moving.

I tried to position myself in the group so that the new lads were behind me, enabling me to avoid watching their ridiculous behavior. However, this proved an impossible feat. Trying to create order in this group was like trying to get battling kittens to walk on strings of yarn. All that interested them was one-upping one another, who could hit harder and mock more meanly.

A quick wind brought a smoky smell. I hoped it was a campfire surrounded by quiet people interested in giving a morsel or two to some weary travelers passing through the area. We walked through a rough batch of budding thistle and climbed a small hill. After we crested the hill, I saw the source of the smoke. Unfortunately, I had been partially right. It was a campfire but it was also our destination.

The fire seemed to be the center of a little hub, with a dozen or so men in small groups dotted around the flames doing chores and saying little to one another. It was not the jovial sight of men drinking to victory that Calum had described. I worried what that meant. A large fellow with long dark hair seemed to be the leader. He was the only one not moving at a quick rate and the only one who yelled instructions to the others.

"Mercy, follow me," Calum said as if I hadn't been following him for more than a day and a half now. "I have to report to Moran."

"Oh, we're coming, too," Girvan said. "No way we're gonna miss this."

All four of the lads descended the hill, which was much steeper on this side than the side we had just climbed, with a child-like hop, skip, run motion. The brothers let out a sort of whoop call as they took flight each time. I feared their kilts would billow out and raise high enough to cause a modesty issue but I was spared that problem by concentrating on my own descent. I chose to retain what was left of my dignity and take the steep hill at a much slower pace, falling more than once, scraping up my hands in the process. I arrived at the bottom a dirty, blood-stained mess but I was satisfied that I had not compromised my self-respect.

"How do you do it?" Girvan asked Calum.

The larger brothers began to walk with slow deliberate steps in a circle around Calum. Ailean, the youngest and smallest stood a bit too close to me for my comfort. I did not like the way the older brothers' eyes changed and the corners of their mouths smirked as they moved. Calum turned as they did, trying to keep one eye on each of them.

"He's nothing to look at," Girvan said.

"Nothing at all," Dugal replied.

Ailean snorted a bit.

"He's hardly charming with all his bumbling about and sputtering," Girvan said.

"He is a bit of a bumbler," Dugal replied.

"Quite a bumbler, I'd say."

"Quite a bumbler, indeed."

"What are you two on about now?" Calum asked, still swiveling his head to keep them both in his sight.

"The lassies, of course," Girvan said. The sneer on his face grew.

"Aye, the lassies." Dugal echoed.

"What lassies?" Calum asked.

"First, Dory, Red Rob's sister's girl with her pretty red hair and her big, blue eyes."

"Green, weren't they?" Dugal asked.

"No matter. And now, this pretty, little priss of a thing." Girvan's head nodded in my direction.

"A priss, no doubt," Dugal agreed, repeating Girvan's motion with his head.

Priss? My mouth opened to object but Calum shot me a look that said to keep my tongue. It took all my energy but I complied, for the moment.

"What about them?" Calum asked. His voice had a stronger tone to it, not by much but it was there. Had he figured out where this was going?

"Dugal and me were wondering, how do ya get them to think ya can help them?" Girvan said. It was not a real question.

"Yeah. How'd ya do it, Calum?" Dugal said and gave Calum a push on the shoulder. Not a shove, but it was not meant to be nice, either.

"It's not as if you look the part of a hero with your puny legs and your wee arms. You probably don't even have hair on your chest!" With this last pronouncement, Girvan let out a hardy laugh which Dugal echoed, to the surprise of no one. Ailean seemed to be losing interest in the encounter and instead concentrated on the flight of a red and black butterfly.

During this odd conversation, the other men in the clan seemed to be going about their work as if Calum was not being harassed. They did not join in the challenge but neither did they make any move to stop it. They simply refused to acknowledge it was happening.

"You already know what happened with Dory," Calum said.

"No, come to think of it. No one does know what happened with Dory, do they Dugal?" Girvan asked.

"Nae. No one knows." Dugal replied.

"She coulda been captured long before you got to Greenock, if you ever did get there." Girvan turned to me for the first time since we had met, or not met to be more accurate. "You know, whatever he told you about being a brave guide, it isn't true. His last charge probably died alone and scared in a freezing dungeon not twenty feet from where he left her."

I never saw it coming. While the final word was leaving Girvan's mouth, Calum lunged at him. How he got his body up to that speed so quick, I have no idea, but when their bodies collided, it was Girvan laying on his back with Calum straddling him. Calum did not keep the upper position for long as Girvan grabbed his attacker's head, used it to roll Calum aside and gain a better position back on his feet.

"Give it up, boy," Girvan teased. "There's no way you'll get the better of me!"

Calum did not give up. He scrambled to his own feet and elbowed his aggressor in the center of the chest which seemed to cause all the air to escape. Girvan bent in half, saliva streaming from his open mouth as he gasped for breath. Calum used this opportunity to hit him with his bare fists directly in the face, first on one side and then the other. Not to be outdone by a lad he had called puny, Girvan blocked a blow headed for his left cheek and somehow turned Calum around so he was facing Dugal, trapped in Girvan's hold. Up to this moment in the physical part of the altercation, Dugal had done nothing, said nothing. Not a thing. Perhaps he was as shocked by it all as I was.

"Come on!" Girvan ordered. "Hit him!"

Dugal cocked his fist but before he let it fly, a dagger soared between him and Calum. We all watched as a small, sharp knife sailed within a whisper of Calum's nose and landed but a scant yard from my feet. After ascertaining that no one had been injured, I looked up to see who had thrown it. The large man with long dark hair who had seemed to be in charge stood staring at the group. His arms were crossed, emphasizing his impressive muscles. I assumed he was Moran, the leader that Calum had mentioned. At least, he was the leader for the moment until this mythical Red Rob MacGregor character showed.

"Enough!" Moran said. Girvan freed Calum by dropping the grip on his arms and Dugal's fisted hand dropped behind his back. "If you are done playing games, Rob will be here before the sun goes down and he'll be expecting a meal." His eyes darted over to me. "And he won't be expecting you."

Girvan and Dugal scampered off to find a chore for themselves, punching each other along the way. Ailean had already left the scene. Calum walked over to the dagger and plucked it from the ground. He did not look up at me as he spun around and returned the dagger to its rightful owner, hilt pointed at Moran, the blade at himself. He and Moran spoke in low voices and did not look up at me or anyone else.

As I stood off to the side of their little camp, alone and ignored, I became more and more angry. How dare Calum leave me there like that? He had not properly introduced me to anyone and did not seem inclined to do so with the oversized Moran.

With no present occupation demanding my time or attention, I thought back on the fight between Girvan and Calum. What had the nasty young man said that caused Calum to leap at him with such fierce anger? Something about a girl named Dory, whomever she was.

"Mercy." Calum's call interrupted my thoughts. He waved me over to where he and Moran stood. Chafing at having to obey his command, I complied.

"Sir, I found Mercy amongst the wreckage of her carriage and burning horse at Loch Eirann. The driver and escort were nowhere to be found and left no sign or signal to indicate a notion of returning," Calum said to his superior.

Annoyed that Calum had not bothered to introduce us and to show that I could speak for myself, I gave Moran a polite curtsy. "Pleasure to meet you, sir. I apologize for the unfortunate circumstances."

Moran ignored my gesture and returned his eyes to the dagger still in his hands. "No need to apologize to me. They are not my unfortunate circumstances. Nor my job to resolve them. Red Rob will decide what we do with you when he returns. Meantime, make yourself busy by dressing that hare for his supper. He might be more amenable to dealing with you if you cook him something for his empty stomach." With that Moran and Calum walked toward the men adding wood splints to the fire.

I stood where they left me, dazed by their rudeness. Calum had been so helpful and thoughtful when he found me. Now, around the other Highland men, he was as cold and curt as the rest of them.

All around me men were working hard, getting the make-shift camp ready for their leader's return. Some were creating resting beds with pine straw and greenery. The late spring weather welcomed some bushes, flowers and high grasses but many of them had prickly pieces. The men had to choose carefully, lest they create a bed of thorns.

Since I had no other options, I walked past the growing fire to a lump of fur and flesh that I guessed were the dead hares Moran had mentioned. Having lived in London my whole life, I was not accustomed to seeing game this way. At the markets, hares, ducks, chickens, and other smaller animals were displayed in clean lines, laid out flat and straight, not dumped in a pile where it was difficult to distinguish one from the next. What a distasteful sight! As I reached for what I hoped was the neck of one of the animals, Calum reappeared at my side.

"I'll get it for you," he said. "It's hard to tell what's what when they're all like this."

"Yes," I said.

"Aye," he corrected. "In the Highlands we say 'aye' when we agree. 'Yes' on its own is not considered respectful."

"Aye," I said. "That is helpful to know." It amused me that the savage, wilderness-dwelling Scots had their own ideas of civil behavior. Calum had returned to his polite self, the one I had met and with whom had left the crash site. Perhaps we were far enough away from the others so they would not hear him.

"Do you know how to dress a hare?" Calum asked.

"I live in London, but not in a palace," I said with a sharp tone. "I am capable of making a simple meal."

"I meant no offense, Mercy. I just wanted to be sure." He reached down his leg and came back up with a small knife. "Here, use this."

I took the knife from his hands and began my work. The size and shape of the knife reminded me of the incident with Girvan, Dugal, and Moran.

"Why did Moran throw a dagger at you?" I asked.

"A sgian-dubh,"

"What?"

"A sgian-dubh," Calum explained. "It's a small dagger you keep in your sock for cutting and eating and," he gestured to the hare in my hands, "whatnot."

"Why would I care what it is called? Knowing to use 'aye' and not 'yes' is helpful but what possible use is it to me to know that this knife is called a skee-an doo?"

"Because if Moran had intended to hurt us, he would have thrown his sgian-achlais."

"His what?"

"Sgian-achlais. It's a weapon you hide in your clothes. It's used to wound whatever or whoever is getting in your way. He threw his sgian-dubh to stop the fighting, not to hurt us."

"That does not explain why I should know what they are called." I said.

"Knowing the difference in the knives means knowing the difference between friend and foe," Calum said. "Putting your weapon on display, like a sgian-dudh, is a sign of trust. Keeping one tucked away, a sgian-achlais, is not."

"But Moran has both."

"Most Highlanders do."

Chapter Thirteen

C alum and I worked together for some time in silence. I was trying hard to figure out how he had come to be with these men, none of whom seemed a bit like him. Nor *to* like him as no one had greeted him upon his return. When I was sure none of them were near enough to hear, I asked him the question that nagged at me the most.

"Are these men your family?"

"Now they are," he answered. It was not a satisfactory answer. I wanted to press him on it but that did not appear to be the wisest course of action. I changed tacks.

"Who is Dory?"

The skillet he held slipped from his grip when I said her name. It hit his foot with a loud *pang!* and Calum had to bite his hand to keep from yelling.

"Sorry," I said and bent over to pick it up.

"My hands must be slippery from the hares' blood," Calum said once he was able to speak again.

It was an obvious lie, an excuse to avoid the topic. This time I decided to press. How could the name of one person cause such reactions?

"No problem," I said. "You were about to tell me about Dory."

"How did you learn that name?"

"Those mean boys, er men, er lads said it right before you knocked one of them to the ground."

"Oh, right." He did not say anything further but became obsessed with laying out the pieces of meat for roasting.

"Who is she?" I asked again.

"A lassie from my old village."

"Were you sweethearts?"

Calum mouth formed a small smile which he tried to hide, then shook his head a bit.

"Nae," he said, "but we were friends. After our village was attacked, it was my job to escort her to safety."

So this was not Calum's first time as an escort in the wilds of the Scottish Highlands.

"After Dory and I went in separate directions, I called insults out to the Redcoats to get them to follow me. I wasn't terribly success-ful as most of them continued to follow her but that didn't stop a few from trailing me with muskets firing. I could only hope the others didn't catch up with Dory."

Calum continued to help as he spoke but only part of him was there beside me and the hare carcasses. Part of him was back in that moment, running for his life, fearing for his friend.

"Bark exploded off tree trunks behind me as I ran a serpent's path through the heavy growth, winding back and forth. I had no idea what direction I was headed as my primary aim was not a certain location, rather to survive with my life and limbs intact."

Calum was quiet for a few moments. I thought perhaps he had fin-ished his tale. I was about to ask a question when he continued.

"The chase lasted for hours that first day. I hid behind boulders when I could find them, in order to catch my breath. Rest lasted a few moments at a time then the relentless Redcoats would call out to each other, giving away that they were drawing nearer. I ran and rested and ran until the sun was gone and thick clouds cloaked the moon. The soldiers had to stop and make a fire for torches so they could see their way back to their commanders. I was proud that they would be returning empty handed, that is, without me in hand."

Calum was no longer helping. He stood still, hare pieces still in his hands, staring at the woods beyond me.

"There was no way to tell when I was safe from the soldiers. I would often hear them marching in the distance but did not know if scouts were scouring the brush and woods looking for me. I would walk as far as I could from dusk until dawn, resting and searching for food and water in the daylight hours."

"When did you sleep?" I asked. We had finished the task of removing the meat from the bones and tendons, I set about cutting the larger pieces into smaller ones the men could skewer with sticks and roast over the fire. Calum seemed to release his stare on the woods and join in my task without thinking, rearranging the meat pieces by size as I cut them.

"During those long, lonely nights I would think of my parents. They died trying to protect me. I lived, but why? My father was an expert tanner and my mother made the most delicious meat pies anyone had ever eaten. What did I do, other than mess up all the time? Getting Dory to Greenock was the most important thing I had ever done and at the time it seemed like it was the reason I had survived. I started to think that if the soldiers were still hunting me maybe they should succeed. Hadn't I already accomplished what my parents gave their lives for? But then, no one came."

I wanted to interrupt with some words of encouragement but none came to mind. Why could I not think of anything to say? Calum was not rubbing his hands on the sides of his head but he still looked like his head ached. I took some feverfew out from my satchel that I had gathered along our travels, weaved the stems together, and handed it to Calum. He took it and chomped down on the heads without a word. He took a drink from his canteen before continuing his tale.

"I stayed in the same camp for days and no one came. Finally, I figured there was something else I needed to do. I knew there was nothing left for me in Glencoe, other than to be pushed around by those fools, the Henderson lads, but where else could I go? Sure, John would protect me, but I was ready for more. I was ready to help and contribute to a community."

"The next morning, I started out in the direction of Glencoe, hoping my purpose would find me before I got there. It took many nights but then it did."

"What did what?" I asked, confused by the turn in his story.

"My purpose found me." For the first time since he started the story, he looked me directly in the eyes. "Some MacGregor men found me while on a scouting trip and brought me back to Red Rob. I had met him in Glencoe once when he visited Dory's mother, who was his sister. They were not close but Red Rob keeps connections everywhere he can and having a sister whose father-in-law was the chief of an important clan in a crucial location was a connection worth keeping. Not a kind man but not unkind either. He doted on Dory. Her rebellious streak entertained him and he fostered it when he could."

"He was glad to see you then?"

"Not at first. He didn't remember me but after telling him my firsthand account of what happened in the glen, he believed I was who I said I was. When he found out I escorted his niece through to Greenock, he laughed with such fervor, the trees tremored."

"He is easily entertained, this man." The task of dressing the hare was complete but Calum was not through with his story. I continued to fuss about, moving the pieces around as if their positions mattered. I wanted him to keep talking.

"Don't say that in front of him. Once he and his men had finished mocking me they all decided that little Dory had escorted me through the wilderness and then wisely cut me loose when I became a problem. Nevertheless, I had succeeded in my mission and that was to be rewarded. Red Rob offered me a choice. I could be taken back to the glen to help rebuild or stay with them and help with their missions. His men were horrified when I chose to stay. I believe Red Rob was surprised, too."

"Did they not know? About your parents?"

"I doubt it and they didn't ask. At that moment, I became an actual outlaw but at least I was a part of something. They always give me the worst jobs they can, but at the end of the day, I've earned my cut of meat same as the rest. I even run missions on my own from time to time."

"Is that why you were out all alone when you found me. How is that being a part of something? Although, I do not blame you for not wanting to be with these men."

"I am with them, even while apart from them. My job out there helps them do theirs. There is no way that they could skulk about in the darkness scouting and rustling if I were not in place as their sentry."

Calum's way of thinking confused me. He knew the men used any opportunity to be rid of him by sending him on these sentry missions but felt that somehow made him part of the group. He had also said his old village would have accepted him back where he could contribute to the whole. Yet, he chose to stay in the wilderness. It was not the way I would choose to live if I had a choice.

Chapter Fourteen

Red Rob MacGregor was not what I expected. Calum's willingness to bend to the wishes of this man whom he does not respect led me to believe Red Rob would be a grand leader. I imagined a tall, broad shouldered man with flowing dark red hair and eyes the color of molasses. My mind's eye could see the plaid draped across his shoulder and gathered at his waist with his strong tree-trunk legs steady beneath the hem of his kilt. The man now standing before the clan was not any of those things, save the color of his hair. He was not particularly large or slight, not tall nor short. His eyes were hazel-green and he wore a mustache, which surprised me. His plaid kilt draped on him as it did all the other men.

Despite my disappointment in his looks, his demeanor was that of a leader. From the moment he was spotted cresting the hill, the men in camp competed with each other to get his attention. It took little time for him to traverse the steep hill, much like Calum, Girvan, Dugal, and even Ailean had done, and be by the fire, roasting stick in hand. He roasted his own meat, of course, but everything else was handed to him before he could even ask.

Calum stood with me and we stayed as close to the shadows as we dared. He did not want MacGregor to notice me before he had eaten. I stared longingly at the fire for the evening air was chilly and the winds were once again picking up force. The delicious smells of roasting hare were almost unbearable and I was anxious for our turn to eat. As I stared at the fire, I noticed buckets of water near the fire and a few by the make-shift beds.

"Calum," I whispered. "Where did the water come from?"

"The loch," he answered, also in a whisper.

"What loch?" I already knew that 'lochs' were what the Scottish called lakes. I had not noticed one near the camp.

"It's on the other side of those trees. Did you not see it from the top of the hill?"

Obviously I had not or I would not have had to ask the question. I did not respond. Instead we sat on my light shawl on the ground, listening to MacGregor's tales of glory, interwoven with times of merry-making, and the connections he made along his travels. At one point he instructed Moran to open the sack he had carried with him. With the flourish of a street performer, Moran produced two loaves of bread from MacGregor's bag. The men cheered with glee and admiration of their leader.

"When you speak to him, remember to limit the amount of English in your voice. Try to say 'aye' and do not talk back to him. His answer is final."

"But what if he refuses to help me?"

"We will have to hope that does not happen."

Calum had said 'we' as if his fate with MacGregor was now somehow tied to mine. For the first time it occurred to me that by bringing me to this place, to his home, Calum had taken a risk, the biggest one he could take. He had risked being removed from the group, kicked out of the clan if MacGregor did not like what I had to say or how I said it. Why would he do that? Why would he place in peril the one thing he valued?

"Wait here," he said. "I'll go roast us some dinner."

I pulled my cloak tighter around my shoulders and hugged myself, trying to melt into the shadows so no one would mention I was there. It was an odd feeling, trying to hide. My uncle had not treasured my existence in his life but he had never made me feel as if I had to pretend I was not there. Doing so now was awkward in a way I had not experienced.

The weight of importance on my conversation with MacGregor

was now enormous. Not only did I have to try to convince him to help me find a man whom I did not know and who was in a place I could not name, all before midsummer but I had to be careful with my words so MacGregor would not deprive Calum of belonging to a clan for the second time in his short life. My knees became shaky and I was no longer sure I wanted to eat.

Calum returned quicker than I expected but I was relieved to see him. My shaky knees and nervous stomach did not stop me from devouring the delicious hare meat Calum had roasted for us. It was a small portion but it filled my belly enough to ease the headache I had been battling all afternoon. I was grateful for the bread as well, though it was stale. Calum even had a cup of cider for us to share. As I sipped, I realized that he had taken his rightful share of the meal and split it between us. He had to be as hungry as I was and he could have eaten his portion and let me beg Red Rob for some of my own but instead he shared without hesitation. This thought made me soften for a moment, then it reinforced my determination to do right by Calum and my family. I felt ready to talk to Red Rob MacGregor.

"When do we speak to him?" I asked.

"Wait," he said. "You must be patient. Moran knows you are here."

"Yes, uh, I mean aye, but does MacGregor know?"

"Of course, I do." That was not Calum's voice. By the look on his face, I could tell Calum had not been expecting anyone else to hear us, either. The speaker, of course, was none other than Red Rob MacGregor himself.

"Come on, then," Moran said on behalf of the leader. "Let us hear your tale of woe."

Hearing my current circumstances called a tale of woe was insulting. As an accurate description, it was also depressing.

I stood up and approached the area where MacGregor and Moran were sitting next to the fire but not too close. I tried to remember all that Calum had taught me but was not sure how to keep the English out of my voice and be loud enough for them to hear me.

"Aye, sirs," I began. I could see Ailean, Girvan and Dugal out of the corner of my eye, nudging each other. "I need assistance to find a man called Mr. Silver."

"Mr. Silver?" Moran asked. "Does he have a first name?"

"Aye, Kingsnot, sir."

One of the three brothers snorted and several of the men snickered. I assumed their juvenile reactions were due to my pronunciation of Mr. Silver's first name. It was difficult to say 'Kingsnot' without running the 's' and the 'not' together.

"What makes you think any of us knows this Mr. Silver?" Moran asked. MacGregor stared at me but said nothing.

The crowd of men were impatient with my story, already. I could not see much but I could hear them rustling around and murmuring to one another.

"I have no direct reason to believe you know him." I was speaking too much and my accent was showing. I tried to hide it but knew that I could not. "I was on my way to meet with him on an important matter when my carriage was destroyed in an accident. One of your men happened upon me and offered assistance. But not knowing my exact destination, there was little he could do without your guidance."

"Your attempt at flattery is –," Moran was unable to finish his thought as MacGregor raised his hand to stop him. "Right," Moran continued. "What business do you have with this mysterious Mr. Silver?"

"I have a critical message that he must receive before midnight on midsummer. It is of the upmost importance that I reach him in time."

"Midsummer? Who do you think you are, Edward Bruce?"

I could not see for sure, but I believed it was Girvan who shouted out the question. His quip roused full out laughter from the group and the low murmuring became side conversations. I had no response and was frightened that the distraction would cause MacGregor to move on to another topic. I had to have help now. Not only did the fate of my mission depend on it but Calum's future would also be affected. Calum had put his trust in this man and in my ability to get him to help me. Us.

To my relief, MacGregor once again raised his hand to signal quiet.

"A message from whom?" he asked. His use of correct grammar stunned me for a moment the length of a heartbeat.

That was a complicated question. "My parents, sir." While not exactly true, it was close enough. There was no reason to try to hide my accent now. I was glad Calum was behind me so I could not see his face. "Please, sir. I have nowhere else to turn and no idea what to do if you cannot help."

"All you have is the name Mr. Silver and somewhere in Scotland?" he asked.

I nodded. "Aye, sir." Hope was draining from my body.

MacGregor looked at me for what felt like an hour but was likely a few seconds. The look in his eyes was strange. Not knowing him well enough to make an accurate judgement, I had to guess it was a look of sadness. When MacGregor asked no further questions and made no movements, Moran spoke.

"Right. Sit down, Mercy." he said. "Who else has business?"

There were mumbles throughout the crowd. One of the men began talking about his situation as I stood still, unable to understand what had happened. Calum tugged gently at my elbow and I allowed myself to be led back to the spot where I had eaten. Eating seemed so senseless now. If I could not get my message to Mr. Silver by midsummer, I would have failed to complete my family's destiny. The thought made me shake.

Chapter Fifteen

"I do not understand," I whispered, once I could remember how to speak. "Why will he not help me? Is it because I offered nothing in trade? I can cook and gather food. I will learn to hunt. I could be a spy, go into villages and chat up the women folk as we do laundry. Everyone knows washer-women are the biggest gossips. I would come back after midsummer to repay my debt by doing all of these things. I can repay him, if he would help me."

"Hush, Mercy," Calum said. "He didn't refuse you."

The scene ran through my mind again. Did I miss the part where he said he would help?

"What do you mean?" I asked being sure to whisper since MacGregor had been able to hear us before. "I did not hear him say he would do anything to assist me."

"He didn't say he would help. But he didn't say he wouldn't. We will have to wait and see if he calls for you later."

"Later? When, later? I have to be wherever it is in scant more than a fortnight."

"Midsummer is almost two fortnights away. Your request can wait another day."

"Another day?" Anger flushed my cheeks but I took a deep breath as I tried to remind myself that Calum had taken a risk as well. I had to remain calm. What would cause MacGregor to wait before giving me an answer? Perhaps he did not want the clansmen to know that there was an important connection whom he had not met. That made sense but did not bode well for me. Or perhaps he simply needed some quiet time to search his recollection for such a man and when and where he may have made a connection with him. Yes, uhm, aye. That made sense.

"Fine," I answered. "I suppose another day will not cause too much more trouble."

The rest of the evening was much like the beginning. After MacGregor had listened to issues concerning scouting territories, disputes over disrespectful comments and actions, and granted time for one of the men to visit his wife and children, the time was passed with stories from MacGregor himself.

"Some of the men have families elsewhere?" I whispered to Calum.

He nodded. "Even Red Rob."

That surprised me. If they had wives and children, why did they not live together in a home? Was cattle-rustling and scouting for MacGregor that much better than farming or being a merchant? Was it what Calum had said, they believed this was their place in the world? It was all so odd to me. I could not understand their thinking.

When it appeared the evening's gathering was over, Calum and I began to prepare ourselves for the night. We stayed seated and pulled what was left of my belongings from my small satchel.

"Mercy," a voice said behind me. I turned to see Moran. My stomach clinched and I could barely breathe. Had he come to tell me MacGregor would help? Did he have the answer to my problem?

"Are you a healer?" he asked.

Startled by the question, I stammered. Calum was quick to answer for me.

"Aye, yeah." He meant to sound casual about it but there was an urgency in his voice that showed his true feelings. Perhaps he thought they were asking for a trade. My knowledge of plants for assistance from MacGregor.

"Why do you ask?" I asked, adopting the casual tone Calum had tried. We continued to shift the items from the satchel around as if this conversation did not require our full attention.

"Girvan saw you giving Calum daisies to eat," he answered. "I have an ache."

Calum and I gave up our pretense of working. I felt confident that I could help Moran and then MacGregor would help me. Us.

"Sure," I said. "Have plants helped you before?"

"Aye, but my supply ran out."

"What did you try?"

"Ginger root. I would boil it and drink it. That usually worked."

Worry crept into my chest as I may not be the kind of healer Moran expected. I did not carry supplies of plants and herbs with me. Instead, I used my knowledge to find the right plants at the right time. In my head, I ran through all the uses of ginger. The most likely problem that ginger tea would ease was upset stomach.

"I see," I said, pretending to take a long time to figure it all out. I furrowed my brow, twitched my mouth to one side and tapped one finger on my right hand into my left palm. Calum started to look worried at my hesitation.

"Aye, fine," I said after at least a full minute had passed. "There is no ginger root here but I will make you a different hot drink. I need a little time to find what I need."

"Aye, right." Moran said dismissively and walked back to supervise the evening watch.

"Can you help him?" Calum asked in a whisper.

"Of course," I said. "As long as I can find the right plants."

"What should I look for?"

"Dandelions. They are easy to spot. I will have to try to find everything else while you boil some water."

I knew where to go to get the right plant for Moran to replace the ginger root he had been using. Calum had mentioned a loch on the other side of the thick tree stand so I headed through the trees to where the ground would become damper. When I started to see ferns, I knew I was close. Queen of the Meadow could not be far away. I caught sight of the tall reddish almost purple colored flowers standing bravely among the greener, lower plant-life. I quickened my pace toward it then heard a strange sound.

Ooooooo.

It sounded like a large creature bellowing.

Oooo. Oooooooooo.

I could distinguish more than one pitch. Were there several large creatures bellowing? The sounds of chomping and chewing soon followed. The lochs of Scotland were known for having terrible creatures living in them. The creatures were called kelpies, water-spirits, water-horses or, worst of all, monsters.

Had I wandered into the den of one such creature? Was I about to fail my mission by becoming a monster's meal? A sudden smell made me turn my head away from the direction of the sounds. It was awful, enough to make me gag and fear that my stomach would eject my meager meal. It smelled like... What a minute, I knew that smell! That disgusting stench reminded me of the large animals that came to market and pulled carts in the streets.

I looked more closely at my surroundings. The large hillock covered in grass near the water's edge moved. Then it mooed. Cattle! MacGregor's men were cattle-rustlers, of course they would have cattle nearby. Large mooing, chewing, horrible-smelling, hairy creatures called Highland cows. Scots called them coos.

Relieved to not have to fear for my life, I resumed my initial chore. I gathered stalks, stems and flowers of the Queen of the Meadow. On my way back to camp, I saw another herb that would be helpful but did not think Moran would like it. I snapped off a small bit and tucked it in the waistband of my skirt. By the time I emerged out of the thicket to the camp side, Calum was pacing like a worried mother hen.

"Did you think a monster had devoured me?" I asked to amuse myself.

"Wrong loch," Calum said with a rare grin. "The water should be boiling by now."

"Fine. I have what I need to prepare the tea."

"I hope this works. It may be the only way to get Moran to help us."

"If he or MacGregor knows Mr. Silver, how would it behoove them to keep that information from me?"

"I don't think they do know him. If they did, they would have asked you for a trade without hesitation. Being Highlanders, they cannot ask for a trade if they do not know their side of the trade to be genuine. My guess is they are weighing which contacts they have that might be able to help and what they want in exchange for that information."

Calum's explanation made no sense to me. If they had information that would help, why would they not share it right off? If there was a deal to be done, set the terms and start negotiations. Why mull it over?

"Do these need to go in the cup in any special way?"

Calum asked the question so sincerely, I almost felt sorry for him.

"Are all Highlanders as ignorant of plants and herbs as you?"

"Not all," he answered, unruffled by my insult. "We have healers."

"Are you out in the wilderness without healers most of the time?"

"We can always find one in the next village. What else do you need to make the tea?"

"Nothing but some space," I answered.

I removed the colorful flowers, braided together the stems and stalks, then placed them all in the cup. Making sure Calum was not looking, I pulled the other small plant from the waist of my skirt and placed it on top of the flowers before covering it with Calum's dandelion. Then I carefully poured boiling water over it all. When I was satisfied that it had steeped long enough, I handed the cup to Calum.

"This should help Moran," I said.

"Right," he said. "Let's go."

Moran was giving orders to men who were already hard at work performing the tasks he was assigning. It was clear he was in a terrible mood. I hoped my tea would help him.

"Sir," Calum said, offering the cup. Moran grabbed it from Calum and drew it to his lips.

"Wait!" I said, perhaps a tad too loud. "It is still quite hot."

"That is no matter to me," Moran replied.

"What I meant, sir, is that you should drink it right before falling asleep. I prepared it in the French manner. Rest will improve the results."

"Right," he said and turned to his right. "Girvan, Dugal take first watch!"

Then he downed the tea, plants and all, and headed to his make-shift bed.

Chapter Sixteen

After we left Moran to his easing stomach ache, Calum and I set about making a place to sleep. It would be nice to get a full night's sleep next to a fire with others around to make me feel safer from the wild animals. Of course, some would call these Scottish savages wild animals. I debated asking Calum if he thought it was safe for me to sleep so close to so many men but it sounded conceited, untrusting, and disrespectful. Calum had not let any danger come to me so far. I had no reason to believe he would allow it now. Still, I longed for the comforts of my London bedchamber.

Once the thought of being unsafe from the clansmen entered my mind, it was difficult to be rid of it. I needed to distract myself.

"Who is Edward Bruce?" I asked.

"What? Why do you ask?"

Honestly, could he not answer a question without asking another one?

"Girvan said something about him at the fire. Who is Edward Bruce and what does he have to do with midsummer?"

"You don't know the story of Bannockburn? The battle that freed Scotland from English rule in 1314?" Calum asked.

"That was Robert the Bruce. Not Edward."

"Robert the Bruce and his brilliant strategies won the battle, freeing Scotland for hundreds of years. His brother, Edward, forced the battle by making a deal about a castle near Bannockburn that had to be completed by midsummer. That's why Girvan made fun of you. It is an essential moment in Scottish history."

At the brief mention of midsummer, every Scot in camp understood Girvan's reference to Edward Bruce. I had a private history tutor and could think of but a few fourteenth century events. For certain, these Highlanders knew the history that was important to their way of life.

I busied myself rearranging the few possessions I had left, trying to make a comfortable resting place while I thought about Calum. He was fiercely Scottish, proud from the crown of his head to the tips of his toes. I was...nothing, actually. I had been born French but raised in England due to my parents' deaths. I could not imagine pledging my life to a community of people who lived in the woods and stole cattle. To Calum, it was an honor and a duty. Honor. Duty. Those words were more than fodder for a Sunday sermon to Calum. They were words to live by. And he did.

"What did you give Moran?" Calum whispered as we settled. He glanced in the direction of Moran who was resting on his portion of bedded ground instead of barking orders.

"He is much changed since he drank it, is he not?" I asked, pride showing in my voice.

"Aye, he is. What was it? How did you know if you prepared right? I have not heard of the French manner of tea."

"I do not know if I should tell you. You may not approve."

A sickened look came across his face and he began to rub his head by his eyes with both hands again. I worried I would have to search for feverfew in the dark.

He closed his eyes. "What did you do?" he asked.

"Nothing horrid," I assured him. He opened his eyes a bit. "A little trickery, is all. I made a simple tea of Queen of the Meadow and the dandelions you found. Then I added a sprig of mint. Nothing dangerous. I made up the French manner business to make it seem more genuine. Sometimes, getting a person to concentrate on something else helps give the plants time to work. There are healing properties in the Queen of the Meadow and the spearmint assists digestion, which is what I think was bothering Moran, and the dandelions help with overall health. Plus they add a nice color."

"You made it sound like you had concocted a near poisonous combination that had to be drunk in a certain manner so as not to put his life in danger. Why would you not tell me the truth?"

"I knew that in order to pull this off, you had to believe me as well. If you knew it was a trick, you might have given it away."

"I would not!" he raised his voice a bit too loud. Someone tossed a rock in our direction which I took as a request to lower our voices. "I keep graver secrets than that."

Calum was livid at the notion that I thought he could not keep a secret. Could he not see that I was protecting my chance to fulfill my own duty to my family? How could he not understand that? His refusal to be reasonable made it difficult to sleep. During the fitful night, my mind filled with terrible images. Most often I saw a knight, his full suit of armor shined to a bright silver, trying to hide in the woods at sunset. A family crest was emblazoned on his armor but I could only catch a glimpse before dark fell and the knight was gone. My mind was taunting me that I would not fulfill my mission and never get a clearer picture of my family.

Calum was not near me when I awoke near dawn but neither was anyone else. The men had risen before me and were busy with morning chores. I did not want to be ungrateful or appear lazy so I rose, rubbed my sore foot, then reassembled my sad little pack, wrapping myself in both shawls until the sun had time to warm the air. As I joined in doing chores without a word, I vowed to press an answer from MacGregor or move on. I had no idea where to go but I had to get moving again. Even if I had to go alone.

The fire burned low and wide in order to heat oats for a quick morning porridge. Knowing they would need water, I grabbed a pan and headed to the loch. As I worked my way through the last of the trees, I was greeted with a wondrous sight. The early rays of the sun danced along the water's surface making the entire loch glisten like a beautiful jewel of an astounding blue color. I took slow, deep breaths of air that smelled like lilacs, wetland moss, cattle hair, and, some-how, sunshine. Birds flew overhead and the nearby bushes rustled with smaller animals beginning their day or bedding down after a night of hunting. Butterflies, so many butterflies, fluttered about on flowers and puddling in the morning dew. I stood still, taking it all in.

Mornings in London are as dark as the evenings. The putrid air always smelled of human waste, ash, and rotten food. The sound of rustling animals was a warning that toe-nibbling rats were about. Scotland was proving to be the opposite. Beautiful.

"Mercy, Red Rob is ready to talk to you." Calum said as he emerged through the trees. "He doesn't look happy."

Chapter Seventeen

A terrible feeling dropped in my chest. The moment I had been determined to make happen since I awoke had arrived but it felt wrong. Part of me was not ready, yet. Part of me wondered why he had waited so long. Regardless of my misgivings, I dipped the pan in the water and followed Calum back to camp leaving the wondrous scene behind us.

MacGregor leaned against a small boulder with one knee bent, bracing his foot on the rock. The top of his plaid was tied around his torso against the chill of the morning air. Moran was not with him. Calum was right. MacGregor's expression was grim.

"Calum," MacGregor said, "bring the water to the fire."

Without hesitation, Calum took the water-filled pan out of my hands and walked in the direction of the fire where the men were making their small repast. I felt alone and vulnerable. Not that I believed that MacGregor would injure me, more that Calum had been my go-between, my buffer. Another thought nagged at me. Why did MacGregor not want Calum to hear whatever he was about to say?

"Lassie," it took a couple of quick heartbeats for me to realize he was addressing me, not telling me about a Scottish lassie.

"Aye, sir."

"I do not know any Mr. Kingsnot Silver and I cannae think of any circumstances where I have heard the name."

The wind carried the smells of the fire and cooking oats to where MacGregor and I stood. I was quite hungry and the odors did nothing to ease it. Calum had believed his clan leader could help me and I had clung to that belief. Now it had been snatched away and I was left with nothing. No idea where to go, nowhere else to turn. I felt empty. Numb.

I could hear MacGregor was speaking again so I forced myself to listen.

"…disappointed, but I truly have nothing for you. Almost nothing. I do have one suggestion, but Calum will not like it."

I cleared the phlegm from my voice before speaking.

"Calum, sir? Why does it matter if Calum will like it or not?"

"Because he is Calum. Once that laddie gives his word to something, he follows it through. No matter the cost to himself. He promised to help you and he will. Or at least he will do everything possible."

"Aye, sir," I said. His description sounded like the Calum I had met two days prior. "Why will he not like your suggestion then?"

"It means going to the one place he has avoided for some time. Glencoe."

"Glencoe? You mean the village where he grew up? The one that was burned?"

"Aye. The village where his family and friends were murdered in front of him and he ran. Surviving that massacre has left a strange effect on him. Now he feels responsible for everyone who asks him for help."

A flash of anger hit me. "Should he not have run? Was he meant to stay and wait for his turn to be slaughtered?"

"Calm down, lassie," MacGregor said shifting which leg was on the ground and which on the rock. "Of course, he should have run. I'm saying Calum feels guilty that he did. But if he had died in Glencoe, he couldnae have delivered my niece to safety."

"He has never been back?"

MacGregor shook his head slowly. "Never. I asked if he wanted to go back to help rebuild but he said he would do more good out here. I sent another scout to tell Dory's family that he had delivered on his promise, as Calum would not go himself. Truth is, there is not much for him to go back to. The clan would have taken him but with his parents gone, he would have to start over on his own even if surrounded by his clansmen. Not easy for anyone his age but for one who feels guilty for the deaths of family members, in the place they died, it could be near impossible."

I stood in silence as I took in all that MacGregor had said. The smells of breakfast oats and fire turned sour as body odor and urine mixed with them on the wind. Had those smells been there all along?

"What would going to Glencoe do for me?" I asked. "How would that help me find Mr. Silver?"

"The seannachie in Glencoe is one of the best in the whole of Scotland. Not only does he tell the glories and tragedies which pertain to the MacDonalds of Glencoe but he is well-traveled and can share tales from many clans and even other countries. If anyone has a clue to your Mr. Silver, it will be Henderson, the Glencoe seannachie."

Calum had told me of the clan's seannachie when we fought about Aesop's tale. This storyteller could be the one who put me back on the right path. How could I ask Calum to take me back to Glencoe? It would not be fair to him.

"Thank you for all of your assistance," I said, looking MacGregor in the eyes. "I have to go there, sir. There is no choice for me. I must complete my mission."

MacGregor frowned at my answer and rubbed his stubble-covered chin with his rough hand. "I know what you did for Moran," he said. The way he said it sounded more accusatory than grateful. "And I know how you did it."

I continued to look him in the eyes but said nothing. I simply nodded.

"Thank you. He is much more agreeable this morning."

With that, he raised his rough hand off his face and waved it to someone behind me. Before I could ask what he was doing, Calum returned to my side. I did not like how my body relaxed a little when he did.

"Do you want to tell him," MacGregor said. "Or should I?"

Without answering the MacGregor, I turned to face Calum and ask of him something that I knew he did not want to give.

"Your chief has told me that he cannot recall anyone named Mr. Silver from his vast network of connections. Therefore, he believes that my sole option is to seek the seannachie who knows more than any other seannachie in Scotland."

The color drained out of Calum's face so fast I thought he would fall to the ground. It did not seem as though he was shocked, or frightened. More like stricken.

Calum turned to MacGregor, who, for the first time I had seen, had a soft look on his face.

"Glencoe?" Calum said, his voice a mere whisper.

"Aye, son," MacGregor affirmed. "She assures me she is determined to find this man. I believe Henderson is her only chance."

"I need to find him in order to fulfill my duty. My family entrusted me with this important task and I must see it through to the end." I paused, hoping he would look at me. "I will go alone, if you cannot."

Calum was silent and still. My heart beat stronger and louder with every pulse as I waited for a reply. Traveling through the Highlands unescorted would be a Herculean task, one which I had no idea how to accomplish. I had to deliver the message. I had no choice but to try, no matter how much peril I faced.

"Nae."

That was all that Calum said. One word. What did he mean? No, he would not go to Glencoe? Or that he refused to let me go on my own? Did that mean he would go with me or that he would find someone else to take me to Glencoe? What did he mean by that 'nae' and why had MacGregor not asked for an explanation? We all stood in maddening silence. I needed to get moving.

"Calum," I said in a low, calm voice. "Thank you for helping me when you found me at the crash site and for bringing me here. My deadline looms and there is much uncertainty. I have to get moving."

I expected Calum to turn to me and say something but he stood still and stared. I looked up at MacGregor who was looking at Calum, concern creeping across the rugged man's face. Was Calum thinking about what to do? Was he trying to keep composed so he would not cry? Or had he entered some sort of hiding place in his own head where the real world could not reach him?

I had meant what I said, I had to get moving. Midsummer was coming on and I had much to do before that date arrived. I could not wait for Calum to return to us. Without looking at MacGregor, I turned to gather my things and prepare for my journey. Alone.

Before I could take more than one step toward my bags, a hand seized the inside of my elbow.

"Wait." Calum had come back to life, at least in part. Without looking at me or MacGregor he continued. "I'll take you there. You would not last one day on your own."

I opened my mouth to protest but he interrupted before I began and looked at me.

"You know it to be true."

MacGregor clapped his hand on Calum's shoulder but said nothing to him. Instead, he shouted orders and the other men hustled about preparing a journey pack for us. Both Calum and I stood and watched these rough men who had seen and done terrible things, gather their hard-fought food and supplies to give to a young Londoner and her escort, a Highlander they claimed to have never accepted. It did not amount to much, some dried hare, a pouch of oats, and a small pan, but it was enough to mean they would have to do without for a time in order for us to make our journey. They had known me less than a day. Highland hospitality took my breath away.

Chapter Eighteen

Calum and I loaded up with my satchel, the journey pack from the clan, and whatever Calum usually carried. We stood in front of the men who were gathered around their chief. I tried to keep my tears from falling. They were not from sadness to be leaving the clan, nor from fear of the trek ahead, but from the generosity the men showed Calum.

"You are a brave lad," MacGregor said to Calum. "Your people will welcome your homecoming. As will we."

MacGregor's words were a surprise to me. I had thought MacGregor would be happy to be rid of Calum. What surprised me more were the smattering of 'Ayes' from the clansmen. Calum may not have been the most popular among the group but he certainly had gained their respect.

"Aye," Calum replied to MacGregor then turned his head around to the men with a nod to acknowledge their farewell. His chest grew as he took a deep breath then he raised his dagger in the air and shouted.

"MacGregor!"

"'S Rio-" the men called out a response but MacGregor raised his hands to stop them. When he turned back to Calum, he had a strange expression on his face, then raised his right eyebrow higher than his left. Calum's expression changed, too, although it was difficult to put a name on it.

"'S Rioghal Mo Dhream!" he called out.

"'S Rioghal Mo Dhream!" the men called back in excited unison. The now boisterous crowd patted, elbowed, punched each other and chanted the Gaelic phrase over and over.

In the midst of the active clan, Calum nodded at MacGregor and the clan chief nodded in return. Calum walked toward the hill and I followed, the camp and loch to our backs. The clansmen marched a few yards with us in a sort of parade as they chanted and knocked each other around in what was, to them, a loving manner. We could still hear the chanting once we had scaled the hill and began our descent on the other side.

Their voices faded and we walked along in silence. We walked through wooded areas with clearings every so often. It was similar to our first day of walking together. Calum's complete silence bothered me. He continued to pull aside branches and point out divots in the ground so I would not trip but did so without a sound. It felt quite odd and I feared for his state of mind. I vowed to pay more attention to my surroundings and our path. There was no telling if Calum would change his mind about returning to his former home and leave me stranded somewhere in the Scottish wilderness. If that happened, I would need to know my bearings.

We came across a small stream, one Calum would call a burn had he been speaking, and followed it in what I thought was a northwesterly direction. I wondered why we had not encountered anyone else. We were not taking a secret path or keeping off the well-traveled road. Following water was the smartest way to travel because you always had access to refresh yourself. Besides, we were following an actual trail, a path forged by the many people who had traveled it before us. Why was no one around now?

"Where are the people?" I asked. "Clearly someone has been here before. The grass is worn down to the dirt. Why is it safe to walk here now?"

Calum did not respond. We walked on in silence, up a rather steep incline. I grew angrier with every step. I knew he was upset about our journey, so was I. It was no reason to freeze me out.

"If you did not want to bring me, you could have said so," I blurted out as if I had been speaking out loud that whole time. "I would have figured something out."

Calum stopped so sudden and I was walking with so much anger, I walked right into him.

"What are you doing?" I asked. Then he pointed dead-center in front of us. We were on the banks of a loch in the middle of which was a small island covered in trees. When I looked closer, rising out of the mini forest in the middle of the loch was a castle.

"That's why," he said.

I stared at the castle but did not understand why that meant there would not be people about. Shouldn't that mean there would be more?

"Besides," Calum said, "we are still in MacGregor territory. No one will bother us here."

Chapter Nineteen

C alum kept moving along the edge of the water. I longed to be inside the castle. It was nothing grand or even big, in fact I had to strain to see it through the trees, but it had walls and a roof. Oh, to be inside again, inside anywhere. I knew Calum had no intention of going to the castle, after all we had miles to cover before we arrived at Glencoe, but I could not stop my mind from imagining the laird's dinner. I had never been in an actual castle, so I could only guess what it would look like. In my mind, there was a long table piled with over-flowing platters of cuts of meat, roasted vegetables, and tureens of dark sauces. Thick, savory smells of baked chicken, fried ham slices, and beef pies would mix with the sweet scents of biscuits and cakes baking in the kitchen. A huge fire in the fireplace situated alongside the dining table would both light and heat the room with a large land-scape portrait of the loch and castle hung above the flames. What a wonderful vision!

Splat. Splat.

Fat rain drops began to fall, bringing my mind fully back to our hike. I looked at Calum, hoping he would find us cover somewhere, even going to the tree line to find a place where we would not get drenched. Instead, I saw him pull the hood of his cloak to cover his head. I mimicked his actions with my own cloak and sighed. The rain started to come down faster and the winds picked up, blowing the drops into a sharp, angled fall.

My layers of clothing were soaked in minutes. This was particu-larly unfortunate as I had donned both aprons and shawls to protect me from the chill of the upcoming storm. The ones closest to my skin clung to me, making each step more difficult. The rain soaked the ground as well and the bottoms of my skirts became caked with mud, weighing them down and further slowing my progress. Calum kept walking, oblivious to my difficulties. His kilt did not fall anywhere near the ground so he had no such issue with the mud. The rain had to have soaked his shirt to his skin but that did not slow his legs. His constant silence grew even more irritating with the worsening weather.

"Calum!" I yelled to him through the storm. "Can we not stop for shelter from the weather?"

He turned his head in my direction and said something that sounded like 'five minutes' but his voice was not loud enough for me to be certain of what I heard. Five minutes? What would happen in five minutes? We would be five minutes soggier. Perhaps, he knew of a safe place to duck out of the weather that was a mere five minutes away? Yes, yes, that made sense. Calum would want me to say 'aye, aye' instead. The thought of getting out of the weather brightened my mood a tad but did not make it any easier to drag myself through the muck and the mud with my clothes sticking to me.

Calum sort of followed the path of a nearby river, once the loch fed into it, but not exactly as we were sticking closer to the tree line. Since he still was not speaking, I had to guess that he kept us there so we could have cover if someone or something tried to attack us. A cheery thought. Soon the tree line thinned, then faded, then was gone. The rain and wind did the same. In the span of less than a quarter hour we went from slogging through sludge in torrential rain and strong winds between trees and the river to walking in the sunshine in the open fields with the river rushing beside us. It had taken more than the five minutes Calum mumbled about, but not much more.

The sun baked dry the mud on my shoes and skirts. Walking with clumps of dried muck on my clothes was not much easier than when the muck was mud. Calum continued to march ahead of me and not speak.

"Calum," I said to get his attention. "I need to stop and get some of this mud off my shoes. It is making it difficult to keep up with you."

He stopped short, as if he were a horse and I had pulled on his reins. I took this opportunity to look for a stick. I found one with relative ease then searched for a large enough rock to lean on. Luckily, Scotland was full of rocks, big rocks. Leaning my backside on one, I lifted my right foot to rest across my left knee and tried to pry the part-dried mud off of my shoes.

"Do you not want to clear your boots of mud?" I asked Calum as I scraped at the mud.

"Nae," he responded without looking at me. He took a seat on a nearby rock. "Highlanders are used to mud. Since you made us stop, though. I will get my fill of drink and take the opportunity to refill my canteen from the river."

"Will we not be by the river for long?" I asked. More because I wanted to keep Calum talking but it would be helpful information to possess all the same.

"You never know when we will have to go off path," he mumbled before lifting the open canteen to his mouth. "You know, your shoes are going to get muddy again soon."

"I understand," I said, still digging at the muck. "For now, at least, I will be able to keep up with you."

"You're the one in a big rush," he said, taking another long drink.

He was correct about that so I had no reasonable response. I changed the subject.

"What was that phrase you all were chanting as we left?" I asked.

"Left where?"

"Calum," I said as I gave him the same look Ms. Mopley had given me when I asked a question of little merit. "If you do not wish to talk about it, fine."

We were quiet again with only the sound of the stick digging through mud passing between us. Content with the progress on the right foot, I switched positions, resting my bottom on the rock so I could reach the left shoe and not have to put my right foot on the ground. Awkward, but I managed.

"Royal is my blood."

"Pardon me," I asked.

"The phrase you asked about," Calum said, still not looking at me. "It is the MacGregor clan motto. The MacGregors are the children of a 9th century king of Scotland."

"I thought you were a MacDonald," I said. I was thinking more about the task of cleaning my shoes than the conversation. Or cleaning them enough to continue on our journey.

"Aye," Calum said. "So?"

"So you are not a MacGregor by blood," I said. Satisfied with my efforts I picked up Bear Man's canteen and took a long drink of water.

"Aye." Calum sat on his rock and stared at the river. The look on his face was one that I had not seen before. It was not sad or scared or even ponderous. Melancholy was too emotional a word for it. Resigned? Perhaps resigned was the correct word.

It occurred to me that what I had witnessed was MacGregor inviting Calum into the clan. Even after years of working, stealing, eating and living with the MacGregors, Calum could not be considered one of them. Inviting an outsider to say the motto with the clan was the same as adopting him, a grant of full acceptance. Yet, Calum was on his way to his original clan, his blood family. He was a man of two clans and felt a part of neither. I understood that feeling. No wonder he was being so quiet.

Chapter Twenty

True to his word, we did not follow the river completely as we continued our trek toward Glencoe. The terrain was odd, not forest, not field. Patches of green grass that looked as soft as my uncle's polishing cloth carpeted the areas between and betwixt clumps of long, wispy grey-brown grasses that fell over on one another. Mountains and large hills, in varying shades of browns and tans with a few green patches, bumped against each other in what seemed to be all directions.

Footing was difficult to master as all the clumps and spots made for uneven walking, more than usual even for me. We climbed a few small hills but the inclines and descents were barely noticeable, not like the much larger hill near the MacGregor camp.

It seemed trekking through the Highlands of Scotland was not a popular activity as we saw no one else as we walked. My legs were weary and my belly grumbled. I wanted to ask Calum if we could stop for a bite but two things kept me from doing so. First, I wanted to get to Glencoe to figure out how to complete my task. Second, I did not want to disturb Calum. He was returning to Glencoe, the one place he never wanted to set foot again. For a stranger. For me. The least I could do was allow him time alone with his thoughts.

We passed through another thicket of trees that seemed to crop up out of nowhere. Calum held branches and pointed out large divots and raised tree roots. Pointed out, not verbally warned.

To entertain myself and to keep me from thinking about the enormous task ahead, I started to collect some of the herbs and other plants that we came across on our journey. Feverfew for headaches. Comfrey for bruises, scrapes, and good luck with travel. An orange butterfly with black and white tipped wings fluttered by and landed on a thistle, which worked well on general aches. Then I picked a few sprigs of spearmint for small tummy troubles. Beautiful purple heather grew out of every rock grouping and indeed out of the rocks themselves as these plants thrive in unusual, harsh conditions. Heather could calm a cough and more serious stomach issues. My collection yielded a beautiful sight with greens, purples, whites, pinks, and yellows mixing together in my kerchief.

The sun had long passed its peak in the sky when Calum stopped for a moment to go through the journey pack and hand me some of the dried hare the clansmen had given us. We did not stop to enjoy our repast but kept walking as we ate. The thought of the look on my uncle's face if he could see me walking while eating made me giggle.

"What is so funny?" Calum snapped.

"Nothing," I said. He would not appreciate the joke.

"I'm glad you are having such a great time," he said with a sourness that indicated he was not happy at all.

"What makes you think I am happy about any of this?"

"Chasing butterflies, collecting a bouquet of flowers and giggling like a little girl," he said. "Looks like you are having a great time."

"How dare you!" I stopped short as I spoke. Calum spun around to face me.

"I dare because it's true. Do you deny it?"

"I am gathering plants for healing." I spoke with a clear steady voice, making sure not to let my anger show. "Soon your headache will get bad enough that you will need more feverfew. I have many other plants in case something else happens." Calum stared at me as I continued. "And I was laughing because I was thinking of how people at home would be upset at the thought of eating while standing up, much less while walking."

"Right," Calum said. "Keep your mocking of Highland ways to yourself."

"That's not wh--," Calum put his right hand up to stop me and his left index finger to his lips to tell me to be quiet. It infuriated me but the dangers out here were real so I reluctantly complied.

"Oh, you donnae know where I came from, do ya?" the words came in a low snarling voice. "I already know she's English, there's no reason to quiet her now. Let me see both hands. Both of ya."

I put my arms in the air, my herb bouquet and kerchief fluttered to the ground. Calum took two tiny steps to his right, his hands in the air. It took my full concentration but my eyes were able to separate the man from the background of the tree bark and dark leaves. He was short, filthy, dressed in rags and holding a blade to Calum's back. I could not recall the different names at the time but it was a knife and it was sharp and this man looked intent on using it. The man bent down, still aiming the knife at Calum's back with one hand, he patted the side of Calum's tall socks.

"What have we got here?" he growled. "Quite a fancy flask for a young lad roaming the countryside." He weighed Calum's beautiful small canteen in his grubby hands. "Feels full. Must be my lucky day. And your unlucky day!"

He thought this a fantastic joke and howled with laughter, right in Calum's ear. How could Calum stand there and take all of this? Had years of being bullied and put down by the Highlanders made him weak? Or incredibly strong?

Calum looked at me, looked to the side, and then looked back at me. Was he having a fit of some kind? He repeated the motion again and again. He was trying to signal me to do something! But what? I looked at him and tried to shrug my shoulders without moving too much as that might alert the thief. Calum mouthed a word. I had no idea what he was trying to tell me. Ugh, it was so frustrating. He mouthed it again. Gan-dee? My-tee? Can-teen? Canteen? Yes it must be canteen. I nodded slightly to indicate I understood. But did Calum think I could pay the thief to leave us alone? Calum mouthed a new word. O-len. Oh, man?

"O-pen."Too late, I realized I had spoken out loud.

The thief had started to search Calum again when my outburst interrupted him. He stood and put the knife's edge right up to Calum's back, making Calum wince.

"What di' ye say?" he barked.

"The flask," Calum said. "She has to open it for you."

"Open." I tried to sound confident. "There's a trick to it. Do you want me show you?"

The thief looked at me and then back at Calum. Calum's face was wretched in pain, but I could not tell if it was from the knife or from me. Yet, I thought I was doing what he asked. Had I messed this up even more?

"Aye, right, go on." the thief said. "But be quick about it, another storm's coming in." He leaned to the side, knife still at Calum's back and tossed me the small canteen. I thought maybe Calum would attack the thief mid-toss being that he would be a bit off-balance but Calum did not. He stood stock-still, staring at me.

Without any way to get more direction from Calum, I got down on one knee and pretended opening the canteen was difficult. As I did, rain began to fall. Not the fat drops that had begun the storm earlier in the day, these were thin and felt sharp when they grazed my skin. The wind sent them sideways. We went from almost dry after the last storm to drenched in the time it took me to unscrew the canteen's cap.

Craa-aa-aaack!!

Thunder sounded so sudden and so loud my first thought was that the earth had cracked open. Lightning lit the sky within seconds. As the thief looked up, responding to the sudden noise and change in lighting, Calum took his chance, twirled around and landed his fist right in the thief's jaw. The thief did not go down but wobbled to the side a few steps, knife still in hand.

"Hands! Your hands!" Calum shouted.

Once I discovered he was talking to me, I stayed on my knees and put my hands on the ground. Calum pushed the thief into me, causing him to lose his balance and fall to the ground. The impact loosened his grip and the knife fell from his hand. He and Calum stared at each other, breathing hard but saying nothing.

Calum was bigger, younger and smarter than the thief but the thief was much closer to the knife. The rain continued to pour down on us and the wind swirled making the rain seem as if it was coming at us from all directions. Lightning and thunder struck at the same time and Calum used the moment to pounce on the thief. As they wrestled on the ground, both men threw and landed punches. Calum fought with a viciousness that twisted my stomach yet I knew it was necessary. That thought twisted my heart as well.

The two were on the ground grappling and wrestling as the thunder and lightning roared and flashed around us. I ran to where I had last seen the knife but it was gone. With the next lightning strike, I saw a flash of light bounce off the knife's blade somewhere in the middle of Calum's and the thief's arms and legs. I could not tell which of them controlled the knife. I stood there watching, feeling helpless. I had to do something.

Without any grand fanfare, the thief stopped moving. Calum rolled to his back and laid on the ground, letting the rain wash over him.

"Is...is he dead?" I asked. The fear that had been zinging around like lightning inside my body turned sluggish and heavy.

"No," Calum responded. "Unconscious for now. Let's get our stuff and get out of here."

"You are bleeding." I said. I untied the extra apron from my waist and turned to help Calum. I could not believe what I saw. The thief was neither dead nor unconscious. He held the knife above his head, aiming it downward at Calum.

"Calum!" I screamed and threw the apron in the direction of the thief's head. His eyes shifted from Calum to the apron flying toward him.

Without hesitation, Calum dove forward, away from the thief, rolled one rotation and was on his feet, facing his attacker, his own dagger in his hands. He lunged forward, plunging the knife into the thief's arm, the one that held his knife, causing the thief's blade to fall to the ground.

"Agggh!" the thief screamed out in pain.

Calum took another swipe at the thief's leg.

"Go, Mercy! Go!"

I ran. Faster than I could ever remember running, which was not a long list as there was not much cause for me to run in the crowded streets of London. I pushed through the agony in my foot and had to trust Calum was following me. I hoped I was running in the same direction that we had been traveling before the thief stepped in our path.

"Faster, Mercy!" Calum was next to me. He had covered the ground I gained on him in mere seconds.

I did my best to not slow us down. It was difficult to run with all the fabric I had around my legs.

"Left, Mercy! Go left!" Calum called out as he grabbed my arm and dragged me to the right, the opposite of what he had said. I guessed he was trying to trick the thief or any other nefarious people who might be skulking about in the wooded area.

We ran and ran. I thought my lungs would catch fire and my throat was dry enough to be the kindling. I tripped more than once but never fell to the ground. The water rushing beside us slowed to a trickle and then disappeared. Only then did Calum allow us to stop and take a rest. We stood, hands on our knees, snot dripping from our noses, panting for air.

"You stabbed him!" I gasped.

"I sliced him," Calum responded in a calmer tone.

"He is gravely injured!" My lungs struggled to recover from the run and argue at the same time.

"He stabbed me!" Calum yelled back. "He would have stabbed me again, you know, to death. And likely you as well. Besides, he's got my canteen full of water and a whole garden of your herbs to heal him. He'll be fine." Calum turned to the side and spit blood. "Or not."

I did not waste my breath to tell Calum that the knowledge of what herb or plant works in what situation was as important as access to the plants themselves. He would not care.

Calum rummaged through the travel sack he had managed to grab in our escape. Finding his goal, Calum raised the Bear Man's canteen and handed it to me. I took a sip, a little longer than I am proud of, before returning it to Calum. The water felt luxurious on my burning throat and seemed to cool my lungs a bit as well. It was not lost on me that Calum, exhausted, bleeding, suffering from a stab wound, and definitely in pain, had handed the canteen to me first.

Chapter Twenty One

"Took you long enough to figure out what I needed you to do," he complained.

"I am not a mind reader," I countered but there was little anger in my voice. I found it more difficult to be angry at him after his simple act of allowing me to quench my thirst before he quenched his own. Instead, I took the apron I had thrown at the thief, which Calum had been able to grab, and ripped off the hem.

"It didn't take a mind reader to know that I needed you to distract him so I could get my dagger. How was I supposed to get us out of there without a weapon?"

As Calum complained, I set to work dabbing at his cuts and bruises. It would have been more helpful if I had water and even better if I could have made a comfrey compress, but the water was too dear to waste on anything but drinking and all the plants I had gathered were lying on the forest floor with the thief and most of our possessions.

"Ow," Calum said and pulled away as I continued to dab at his injuries. "Good thing you are wearing so many layers and had that extra apron. I grabbed the travel pack and still have most of what I carry. My canteen is gone and your herbs."

"We have the other canteen and I can gather more plants as we go."

"What about your small bag?"

"My satchel?" I dropped the bloody hem on Calum's shoulder as I looked down at myself. I patted my sides and across my chest searching for the strap that had been around my body for weeks. I had never let anyone else handle it, not once. It was far too precious.

I did not find it.

"Aye, yeah, the one you always wear?" Calum asked, unaware of the panic racing throughout my body.

I continued to check around my neck as I looked to the ground and then back down in the direction from which we had traveled. "It is gone."

"Strap must have broken when the thief fell over you," Calum said. "There goes the cash." He picked up the bloody hem and blotted at the wounds on his arms, oblivious to my fear.

"It is gone."

"Aye, I know," Calum said as he studied his wounds. "Like my canteen and your herbs and whatever else we left."

I turned and ran back toward the woods, encumbered by my flapping skirts and muddy ground.

"Whoa, there! Where are you going?" Calum called after me.

"I have to get it back."

Calum hurried past me and stood in my path.

"You can't."

"I have to!" I said and tried to get around him. He stepped in my path again. He placed his hands on my shoulders.

"No." Calum said. "The thief will not hesitate to kill us the next chance he gets."

"I have to take that risk." I stared past him in the direction from where we had come.

"At least tell me why."

I looked him in the face to be sure he heard me. "My only hope of delivering the message is in that satchel."

The wind blew hard for a few seconds making the leaves and grasses rustle and swoosh. They were the only sounds as Calum tried to understand what I had said.

"What? What do you mean? Isn't the message, you know, a message?"

Struggling against his grasp, I answered. "My mission begins by reciting a poem so this Mr. Silver knows whom I am and why I have come. Without the poem, he will not allow me to deliver the message."

"And the poem is in the satchel?" Calum asked. I nodded. "Do you know what it says? Did you ever read it?"

My heartbeat quickened and my stomach churned as the realization of the lost satchel seeped deeper into my mind. My entire body seemed to be sweating.

"Mercy?" Again, when Calum said my name, it distracted me from my thoughts for the length of a breath before my mind returned to the issue at hand. "Have you ever read the poem?"

"Aye," I said, careful to use the Highland word on the first try this time. "My uncle told me to read it every night before bed."

"Fine, then," Calum said. He released my shoulders and blotted his arms with the bloody hem still in his hand. "You know the poem."

"I told you I do not have it any more!"

"You don't need the paper, you know it. You're nervous now, so you may not remember it all, but you will."

"No, I need to get my satchel back."

"Nae."

"Yes."

"No."

"Aye."

I was tired of fighting. I gathered my skirts in order to continue my quest back to where the thief had attacked us. Calum grabbed my arm and spun me to face him. Neither of us spoke. He tilted his head to the right as if trying to read something on my face. I looked down at our feet.

"I have to get it back," I said to the mud. "It belonged to my grandmother. It is the only family relic I know is real."

We stood like that, Calum holding my arm, me staring at the ground, pretending that tears were not dripping from my eyes.

"We can't." he whispered.

I blinked and sniffed six or seven times before I could speak.

"I know."

Chapter Twenty Two

The realization that I had lost my one last tangible connection to my family forever and now I had to continue on not knowing if I could remember the poem word-for-word, made me feel sick and achy inside and out. Calum knowing another piece of information about me intensified the sick feeling. Devastation, irritation, and humiliation fought for space in my mind.

"Let's go. We need to make it to Loch Tulla before dark."

Calum had wrapped the bloody apron hem around the worst cut on his leg and started off in the direction we had been traveling. I did the only thing I could. I followed him.

As we walked, I tried to remember the poem but my mind was pulling me back to the woods and my family satchel. I hoped Calum was right, that I was too nervous at the moment to remember all the words. What would happen when I did? It was not as if I had a way to write it down again. Was this whole trip for nothing? Would I fail the Alliance? Would I never learn anything about my family?

Hills in the distance rolled up against each other in deep green and brown hues. There were some spots of yellow here and there. Small bushes dotted the countryside but none held any plants or herbs useful to me. The grasses where we walked were up to my knees, waving in the breeze but bent in the high winds that seemed to sweep through the area without warning. The winds never seemed to phase Calum or alter his pace in any way. He kept moving, every step bringing him closer to his goal. Our goal. My goal, to tell the truth.

"Are you alright?" Calum asked. I had not been aware that he had been watching me as we walked.

I did not reply.

He pulled out the Bear Man's canteen and handed it to me.

"There is not much left," I said. "We should save it until we can get more water."

"What did you suppose that was?" Calum pointed to our left. In the distance, I could make out an azure color peeking out between fields of emerald green and golden brown. "That's the Orchy. It runs into Loch Tulla. Now drink. I donnae want to have to drag you."

Responding to his insult would have resulted in nothing more than another fight. Instead I took the opportunity to fill my mouth with water from the canteen and be slow to swallow it, enjoying the feeling of the water trickling through my body. When I was through, I handed the canteen back to Calum.

"How long until we arrive in Glencoe?"

"Depends on how long a rest we take. Where the river runs to the loch there are plenty of fish. We can catch a meal, take turns sleeping, get moving before dawn and in Glencoe by supper."

"And then the storyteller will be able to tell me where to go to deliver my message?"

"Seannachie," Calum said. "I hope so. Have you remembered much of the poem, yet?"

I snapped my head in his direction. How did he know that was what I had been doing?

"Like I said, you're smart, you'll figure it out. John will have paper and pen so you can write it down after you get it all. Since you can read, I figured you know how to write as well?"

"My uncle saw to it that I was educated by the finest tutors in our area of London. I know a great many things, including how to read, write, and speak both English and French."

"A simple 'aye' would have done but good for you. Did your tutors teach you how to catch a fish?"

"I have used my uncle's rod many times," I said.

"Aye, yeah, but have you caught a fish without a rod?"

Was that a trick question? I would have snapped back with a retort of some kind but the winds picked up and the sky dropped buckets of water on us without so much as a warning droplet. Rain soaked the ground in seconds and soon I was trudging along in my mud-clogged shoes with my skirts weighed down by sludge. Calum kept the pace steady, as always, with no concessions to the change in weather.

The wind tugged at the edges of my cloak and wrap, whipping the sopping wet cloth through the air and my foot pain intensified but I was determined to keep up with Calum. By the time the wind and rain died down, I was soaked through with rain, but also with sweat. My efforts were rewarded when Calum turned his head to check how far I had fallen back and I was within a meager two steps of him.

As we came closer to the running water of the river, the ground became so boggy that if I stood too long in one spot I would start to sink. We passed more plants that would be of use for me. I gathered comfrey and feverfew and planned to get Queen of the Meadow when we were close enough to the loch.

Although we could see the river, it still took at least a half hour to reach it and perhaps a quarter hour more to reach the edge of the loch.

"Go ahead and get your plants," Calum said when we got close to the loch. "I'll catch dinner."

"You really think you can catch a fish without a rod?" I asked.

"No," he replied, calling over his shoulder, "I know I can."

I searched the area near the loch and gathered many plants, including Queen of the Meadow, and kept them in the hem-less remnants of my apron. As I got lower to the ground to examine the plants, I could see something in the mud.

"Looks like animal tracks," I called out to Calum. He had been searching near the banks of the loch as well.

"Mm-hmm," he said in a way that made me think he was not truly listening.

"They look like big animals," I continued, trying to get his attention. "Like a horse or one of your Scottish unicorns."

"Sure," Calum replied as he waded not into the water but the high grasses near the edge.

"Sure, what?" I asked, my tone a bit nastier.

This time Calum did not bother to reply at all. Instead, he walked deeper into the plant life. He emerged with a few blades of the high grasses but his socks were heavy with prickly burrs.

"Do you need help removing those?"

"Nae. I need them."

Calum dropped the travel pack off his shoulder onto the ground. He untied one strap, rooted around inside the bag and pulled out a line and hook. Gifts from MacGregor's clan. Calum must have known what was in the travel pack. He grabbed one of the burrs from his socks and threaded it onto the hook. He tied that to the line. The contraption looked ridiculous and there was no way it would fool even the dumbest of creatures.

"Calum," I said, deciding not to comment on his fishing skills, "are you not concerned that there is a large animal about?"

"No." He was frowning at his makeshift fishing gear but said nothing else.

"May I ask why not?"

"It's either a unicorn, which is quite unlikely, wild boar, deer or a horse. Those animals will not bother us since we are making noise and will soon have a fire going. It could have been a person on a horse coming through the area. I would expect nothing less. Plenty of people live nearby. Could have been a MacDonald."

His smug self-assurance did not put my mind at ease. I shifted my apron full of plants to my left hip so I could pick a bunch of feverfew. I hoped we would be eating more than what I picked to ease our headaches and stomachs. I was not counting on fresh fish but perhaps the dried hare from MacGregor's men.

"A MacDonald? Is that not your clan? Your old clan, anyway?"

"Why?"

Why? Really? Could he not answer a simple question directly? Why was he so frustrating?

I sighed. Loud. "If MacDonald is your old clan and one of them could have been here recently on horseback, does that mean we are close to Glencoe?"

"I told you before. We should be there before mid-afternoon tomorrow."

Less than a day and I could have the answer to where I needed to go. I set my mind back to thinking about the poem. There was little time for me to remember it. If I could not get the words back, all of this would be for nothing.

Chapter Twenty Three

Calum walked a few steps into the water, wrapped the line around his right hand a few times and tossed the burr-covered hook into the loch. The water trickled under the burr, carrying it a bit as it floated and bobbed. My stomach growled like a weak kitten as I wondered what kind of fish would be daft enough to bite such a creation. Once it had traveled the length of the line, Calum pulled it back to himself, checked the burr was well attached and cast it into the water once again.

I pretended to ignore him and searched for more plants. We had come far enough north that the plant life was a bit different than from where Calum had found me. Thistle, an excellent remedy for aches, were more prevalent here but had to be chosen with care as the pretty purple flowers were protected by prickles up and down the rest of the plant. I looked around at all the trees. From a distance, they looked ghostly, as if covered by a spectral aura. Up close, they appeared to be covered in a series of tiny plants.

"Calum?"

"Aye?" he responded without looking at me.

"What are the plants growing on the trees? They do not appear to be vines."

"You mean there is a type of plant life that you cannae make into a special tea or compress or whatever?"

"That was quite rude." It was a statement, not an accusation. "If you do not know, then tell me that. There was no call for such a nasty response."

"I was surprised that you did not know what it was, that's all." Neither of us spoke as Calum went through his ritual with the burr, line, and hook. Once it was in the water again, he continued. "Crottle."

"Grottle" I asked. Honestly, the lad mumbled at the oddest times.

"No. Crottle. The English call it lichen."

"Lichen? That is used to dye weaving materials which result in impressive colors. I have not seen them look this pale."

"So, no cures, then?"

"Lungwort is lichen and is good for a cough but you have to boil it a long time. I am not well versed in lichen and some are poisonous."

"Right," Calum replied. "Let's stick to colors, then, shall we?"

"How did you know what we call it in England?"

"Red Rob's men travel far and wide."

Calum's rudeness was near unbearable. Was he not capable of a civilized conversation? As I opened my mouth to scold him again, he pulled back hard on the line.

"Got one!"

Calum pulled the line with a quick smooth motion, wrapping the line around his hand to keep the line taut. Soon he was holding a salmon.

"Zounds!" I cried. "I cannot believe my eyes."

"You didnae think I could catch supper?" Calum said more than asked. "Thanks for the confidence."

"I do apologize," I said. "But I still think using a prickly burr is an odd way to catch a fish."

"Not much of an apology," Calum said. "It may look odd but when you survive in the Highlands, how a thing looks to outsiders does not matter as long as it gets the job done. Now, let's start a fire."

"I am perfectly capable of starting a fire for supper," I said. Of course, I had no idea how to start a fire in a field. I had barely been taught how to start a cooking fire in a proper fireplace.

"No need," Calum said. "I'll start it now so you cook this one while I catch another. You can go through the pack and get out the pan."

Minutes later Calum was back to fishing while I tended to the one on the fire. Our little scene felt pleasant, serene even, until I heard a noise. It started far in the distance and came closer for sure. The louder it got, the more certain I was of what it could be.

"Calum."

"I hear them."

"What do we do?"

Calum ran back into the high grasses. For a shameful few seconds, I entertained the absurd thought that he was abandoning me. He returned with two large, thick sticks. He laid one end of each into the fire leaving the other ends pointing away from the flames.

"Torches," he explained. "Let's hope you do not need them."

Calum picked up his fishing gear but stood closer to the edge of the water, no longer knee deep. I thought he would stand near the torches in case he needed a weapon. A glint along the inside of Calum's arm caught my attention. His knife. Probably not the one from his sock.

The once-distant sound grew nearer and nearer. Soon the image of a horse and rider emerged. There was a second rider to his right. Calum tossed his line back in the loch and I squatted by the fire to check our meal in the pan. Calum had his line in the water but he was not fishing. He did not take his eyes off of the incoming riders. When the horses were close enough for us to hear their breath, Calum straightened his shoulders and squared his body to the stranger on the first horse.

A realization occurred to me like a kick in my gut. When he set up the torches, Calum had said 'hope you do not need them' not 'hope we do not need them.' In Calum's mind, he had his weapon, his knife, and I had mine: the torches. He expected me to be able to protect myself.

I had never used a torch as a weapon. I had never used a weapon. What would I do with it? Throw the torches at them? Could they not then pick it up and use it against us? I could not imagine I would use it to injure the horses. Perhaps I could frighten them? Why hadn't Calum told me what to do? Why did he think I knew how to do this?

"Calum?" I asked.

"Aye," he responded without looking back at me. He kept his eyes on the approaching horsemen.

"Is there, um, something specific I should do with the torches?" I felt like a fool asking but what if there was some key information to using torches that I did not know?

"It's fire, Mercy," he answered. "You'll figure it out."

Calum was right, I would. He had faith that I could be of help by using the torches so why should I not have that same faith? No reason. I would figure it out.

"Aye," I said without the slightest quiver in my voice. Bring on the strangers. Calum and I could take them. Right?

The man on the lead horse came into focus. He wore the kilt of a Highland savage with the top gathered and draped across the shoulder of his shirt in defiance of the chill in the evening air. His boots were fashioned from the skin of a light brown animal and fastened with leather straps. He did not have a pack attached to himself or the horse. Nor did the other man. Were they simply out for a ride or traveling light for another reason? A more dangerous one. The lead man bent his head from side to side as if to get a better look us.

"Calum?" he called out when he was close enough for his voice to reach us. Did Calum know this man?

Calum mimicked the man's head motions trying to assess the men.

"Chief?"

Chapter Twenty Four

C hief? Calum said chief. Who's chief? Chief of what? Or whom?
"I cannae believe my eyes!" the man said as he dismounted with
ease. "My son! You've returned!"

The man walked up to Calum and clapped his hands on Calum's
shoulders in a strange embrace. Calum looked to the ground first,
then lifted his gaze to meet the larger man's.

"I was not sure I would ever have the pleasure of seeing you again!"

"Aye, sir," Calum replied, "it is always pleasing to see you."

"Who's the lassie?" the man said with a sideways nod of his head in
my general direction.

How insulting! How dare this man speak about me to Calum instead of address me directly? Before Calum could warn me not to
speak with my English accent, I answered. "I am Mercy."

The chief's eyebrows raised as if trying to touch his hairline. "Aye.
Not a lassie, eh?" He squeezed Calum's shoulders before releasing him,
then turned to face me.

"Are you from London, Mercy?" he asked.

Impressed that he talked to me instead of about me and that he
identified my accent as being from London and not some other part of
England, I answered him with the respect a chief deserved. "Aye, sir."

"Well, Mercy of London, I am John MacIain of Glencoe. Let's catch
some more fish. When a young lady Londoner is in our Highlands
with Calum, there's bound to be a good story, worthy of a good meal."

MacIain's behavior surprised me. The fact that he had a guard,
whose name turned out to be Leith, meant that he was a man of importance, but this man did not act like he expected things to be done
for him. Leith followed his orders without delay but did not hover

about him or make sure he had what he needed. Highlanders had a strange way of treating their leaders. The three men stood in the water, casting their rod-less lines in the water in silence. It had an odd calming effect.

I took the first salmon off the fire and set the pan to the side so it did not overcook. I went back to collecting plants while keeping an eye on our meal to guard it from scavenging animals. I also snuck as many glances at the chief as I could. He had called Calum son but Calum had told me his parents died in the raid on their village. Perhaps this was how Highlanders spoke with one another? Calum had not seemed happy to see his fellow clansmen. Of course, that had to do with the raid, as well.

It struck me as unusual that Calum and Leith did not interact. In fact, Calum had grown silent since they entered camp, save for his initial brief conversation with MacIain. He had not even spoken to me. Why did he not ask them how the villagers were or how reconstruction fared? Why did they not pepper him with questions about his adventures with the MacGregors? Or at least inquire about each other's health? Why did Calum choose to stay mute?

The four of us cooked and ate around the fire as the sun slipped closer and closer to the horizon but it would still be hours before darkness engulfed our little camp. No one spoke. Calum and Leith did not look at each other. There had to be some sort of bad blood between them. I had no idea what nor did it truly matter to me.

"That's quite a scratch you got there," MacIain said to Calum.

Calum shrugged.

The only scratches I remember Calum having were from the fight with the thief. They were not bad at all. Scrapes, hardly worth mentioning. Why would the chief, whose own hands were covered in cuts and abrasions, comment on such small scratches?

"What scratch?" I asked.

Calum shot a look at his chief. It seemed to be a warning of some kind.

To keep quiet, perhaps? His chief nodded in return and turned his attention back to his fish. It was clear Calum would not answer my question.

Whatever history existed among these men was none of my business and I could not let it distract from the true reason Calum and I were there. I needed help fulfilling my mission. Since Calum was not talking, I decided to ask his chief myself.

"Sir," I began since I had no idea the proper address for this man. Mr. MacIain seemed too formal. "I am afraid I must ask of you a great favor."

"A favor?" he asked, glancing in Calum's direction who looked back at the chief but said nothing. "What sort of favor might that be?"

"Aye, sir," I said. He turned his head back in my direction and gave me the full attention of his blue eyes. "I need to deliver a message to a man called Mr. Kingsnot Silver. Do you know him?"

"Kingsnot Silver? No, I donnae know him. I would remember that name. Where does he live?"

"That is the crux of my issue, sir. I do not know. I was traveling there with my chaperone, Mr. Willicks, to deliver a message but we had a carriage wreck and Mr. Willicks is gone."

"Dead?" he asked.

"Deserted," Calum broke his silence to underscore my humiliation. Wonderful.

"He was not at the site when I woke. Calum took me to see MacGregor. He did not know of Mr. Silver but suggested that your storyteller, er, seannachie might. Calum agreed to take me to Glencoe to ask him. Do you think he will help me?"

Both MacIain's and Leith's heads snapped in Calum's direction when I said the name of their village.

"You are coming home?" the chief asked in a flat tone.

"I am fulfilling a mission that brings me to Glencoe," Calum replied.

MacIain and his guard looked at each other but did not comment. Instead, the chief turned to me and answered my question.

"Aye, the seannachie will help you if he knows anything about this Silver. We will ask him when he returns."

Returns? Did he say returns? Calum looked his chief in the eyes and stopped chewing. Fear seized me and I found it difficult to draw breath.

"Is he not in Glencoe now, sir?" I managed to ask.

"Nae, he is out traveling," MacIain replied. "Do not worry, he will not be gone long. Perhaps another few weeks or so."

He spoke in a casual tone, but the devastating effects of his words landed as hard as an actual blow to the face. A few weeks or so? That was past my deadline for sure. I could not wait that long for his return. Even if I had the time for that, I had no guarantee that he would know where I needed to go in order to meet Mr. Silver or how long it would take to get there.

Everything I had gone through, all the training in London, the lonely times I spent wishing for a family while I studied to save that same family's destiny, the terrible trip with the tight-lipped Mr. Willicks, the horrible carriage wreck, the never-ending agony from my deformed foot during my trek with Calum, and forcing him to return to a place he never wanted to see again, it was all for nothing. Nothing. I would fail. I would not deliver the message. I would never know of my family or from where I came. My unsuccessful mission would result in the collapse of the Alliance and the character of the family I longed to know would be sullied forever. My one chance to be connected to a family would be as the fool who destroyed its reputation.

Chapter Twenty Five

The rest of our time where the river met the loch is a blur of vague flashes. Calum putting the MacGregor's journey pack on my back, him wrapping both my shawls around my shoulders, being on the back of one of the horses leaning up against Calum's back as he gently urged the horse to move. My mind could not focus on anything outside of my body for more than a few moments, instead requiring all its energy to try to untangle this mess of a mission.

All the effort and planning could not be for nothing. I thought and thought, trying to come up with a way to save the mission. How could I make this work? How could I figure out where I needed to go or whom I needed to contact? I had to find a way to deliver the message. But how? Maybe there was a storyteller from another clan who could help? Perhaps MacIain knew the direction their seannachie had traveled and Calum would take me to meet him?

Of course, I also had to remember the poem. There were lines running through my cluttered mind but I could not spare the time to straighten them. There was no hope of finishing my quest without the poem. That would only matter if I could figure out how to reach Mr. Kingsnot Silver by midsummer.

My thoughts were interrupted and my mind brought back to my body when the horse trotted into a low dark cloud which turned out to be a swarm of tiny insects.

"Midges," Calum mumbled.

"What are midges?" I asked. "Oww. Are they biting me?"

"Aye. They like the boggy, wet areas."

As far as I could see, all of the Scottish Highlands consisted of a boggy, wet area. It would not be pleasant to be attacked by these crea-tures for the whole time I was in the Highlands.

"How do you combat them?"

"What do you mean?"

"What makes them go away?"

Calum was silent as the horse trotted forward a few steps. "The sun."

I would have to come up with some concoction to keep the nasty little biters off us. Until then, I buried my head in Calum's back. The enormity of my situation overwhelmed my brain. If there had been enough mind-power to give to my eyes, I might have cried. Instead, I fell asleep.

Sleeping on the back of a horse is tricky business. I had to hold on to Calum's waist to keep from falling off, keep one ear against his back and the hood of my cloak over my head. It meant I could hear every breath he took, when his breathing was easy and when it shuddered. Listening to it became a kind of lullaby and I do believe I slept for quite a few miles. I awoke when his breathing changed. It became deeper and slower, more deliberate. I assumed that meant we were getting closer to his former home, the place where his family and friends had been slaughtered and their homes burned. A place he had never want-ed to go again. He was going back because I, a stranger, needed his assistance. And now, going back might not be enough to save me.

"You awake?" he asked.

"Aye, yes, aye." Would I ever get used to the Highland words? Would I be here long enough for it to matter?

"We are close to the baile. John will make sure we have warm, dry beds for the night."

I was grateful at the thought of a regular warm bed next to a fire but why had Calum mentioned that it would be dry as well?

As I opened my mouth to ask what he meant, the first fat drops of the next rain storm landed on the only exposed skin I had, my arm between my wrist and elbow. I knew it was worthless to try to continue the conversation. The rain would soon be pounding down on us and the horses, making the trip more difficult and the noise too loud for talking. I buried my head in Calum's back again and waited for the rain to stop.

It did not stop, at least not at the interval I had come to expect from Highland weather. As the rainfall got even heavier and we could hear thunder in the distance, the horses began to react. They whinnied and slowed their pace. Apparently, they were not as stoic about the foul weather as their Highland riders. Or perhaps the horses, like me, had anticipated a shorter storm.

I must have drifted back to sleep because the next thing I remember was Calum speaking in a quiet tone, asking me if I was awake. Embarrassed that I had been caught sleeping, although for what reason I cannot tell you, I replied in a sharper tone than necessary.

"Yes, yes. Aye." I sighed loudly to give my mind time to catch up. "I am awake." I pulled my hood back and realized the rain had stopped. I could see smoke rising in gentle even columns. "Is that the village?"

"Baile."

"Pail?" I asked, watching my tone this time. It was clear, at the least the foreseeable future, that I would need to make an effort with Highland language. "Like a bucket?"

"Nae. Baile. B-b-baile. It means village."

"Aye, yes. Fine."

I looked around us for the other horse carrying MacIain and Leith. They were in front of us and off to the left. The formation was similar to the one Leith took upon their discovery of us by the river and loch. The men of Glencoe were protective of their chief. According to what Calum had told me, they had every right to be.

"What will happen now?" I asked. "You heard what your chief said.

How will I find Mr. Silver if we cannot even find the storytel – I mean, seannachie?"

"We will sleep, Mercy. All we can do tonight is sleep."

He was correct, of course, but it did not stop my heart from worrying.

Chapter Twenty Six

I must have slept through the early parts of the change in terrain. Huge hills topped with rocky peaks surrounded us on all sides. My neck ached as I angled it to see the tops. The green of the hills against the greys and browns of the crags created a strange combination of muted and keen colors. The great mountains rolled into one another in soothing strokes. As massive and imposing as it looked, when we rode deeper into the landscape, it felt like a welcoming embrace.

The closer we rode, the more details emerged. Purple, pink, yellow, and gold plants dotted the landscape. Tall, spindly tree trunks stood side by side growing to impossible heights and seemed to act as guardians for the greener trees behind them. The view in every direction was breath-taking. I understood why people would choose to live here, even with all the hardships involved. In London, everything was grey. Everything.

Calum had to be feeling a storm of emotions as we entered his former village, or baile, as he said. Fear. Confusion. Anger. Bitterness. Guilt. What will it look like? Were there still burned out shells where homes once stood? How would the others react to him? Did they resent him for surviving when others had not? Did they think him less honorable because he had not helped with the rebuilding? He cherished his Highland sense of honor beyond what I could understand. This beautiful place was now haunted by the memories of his entire family, his friends and fellow clansmen being slaughtered. Calum did not want to return. He felt duty-bound to do so. For me.

Before the buildings were visible, when only the smoke columns that rose from them could be seen, several young men came along the path to meet our party. Clearly the MacDonalds had scouts like

MacGregor's men did. It must be commonplace in the Highlands to spy on one another. The young men, each within a few years of Calum's age, dressed similar in that each had at least one part of their outfit made of the same tartan pattern. Most wore tartan kilts as Calum, MacIain, and Leith did. They ignored us and our horse, concentrating instead on welcoming their chief and his guard. It was not until we were near the buildings that one of them looked back at us.

"Calum?" one of them asked. Most of the others snapped their heads in our direction. Well, Calum's direction.

From my position on the horse behind Calum, I could tell that we had not changed pace nor had he raised a hand in greeting. I could not see his face but guessed that his expression had not changed either.

"It is Calum!" another one called. Three of the young men took off at a fast run in the opposite direction, back to the baile. Four or five of the ones who stayed came closer to us.

"Why are you back?"

"Where have you been?

"Did MacGregor finally kick you out?"

"Is he as intense as they say?"

"Did you learn anything useful?"

"Were you his bucket boy?"

"Who's the lassie?"

"That's enough, lads," the chief said. "We have a guest in need of water, nourishment, and rest. Go make preparations!"

I could see more questions on the young men's faces but they only hesitated for a second before running back to the village.

MacIain stopped his horse and allowed ours to come astride.

"I will not allow them to badger you again tonight. You need rest. Tomorrow we will reunite you with your clan."

Either the clanspeople fully respected the chief or the next rain storm kept them away. We were allowed to eat, drink, and fall into beds without being asked another question. Whose food we ate, drink we drank and beds we slept in, I did not know, nor did I care. I cherished the warm, dry straw mattress beneath me. The winds blew hard against the walls, the rain drummed down on the roof, but a fire crackled in a fireplace giving the small home a wonderful warm feeling. Before my mind gave way to a deep sleep, I pledged to myself to fulfill my quest and retain my family's honor. Calum would. In fact, he was doing so right now.

Chapter Twenty Seven

Sleep came easy but so did the dreams. The same dreams I had had my entire life used to frighten me. I would wake up to my own screams and no one would come to check on me. Without parents, I learned to console myself and that nightmares cannot hurt me.

This time, I did not awaken to the sounds of screams, my own or anyone else's. Instead, I woke to the sound of soft humming. It was confusing at first. At home, I woke to the loud noises of the bustling city. Since being on the road, the sounds of inn proprietors beginning their days of serving and cleaning greeted me each morning. The quiet humming disoriented me.

I opened my eyes trying to ascertain from where the humming emanated. Calum was nowhere to be seen. It was jarring how awkward I felt when I realized he was not within eyesight. I felt concern, but for him or for me? Strange how quickly I had become dependent on him. Especially considering how annoying he could be.

My surroundings came into focus. It was a home, neat and organized. Furnishings were solid-looking but scarce. There was a large section separated off in what I would call an animal pen. Did the animals sleep inside with the clanspeople? That would explain the strong smells.

In the rest of the home, stood a simple table, a chair on each of the four sides, a long chest on the floor and a small cabinet, the bed I was lying on, the other where Calum had slept, and a third under a small window. Around the hearth hung a pot, a pan and a poker. It was so simple, I could not tell how many people lived here.

The door opened and a lovely, tall woman entered the space. She was the source of the humming. She moved about the home with ease, stoking the fire and restocking the wood pile. The shawl she wore wrapped around her shoulders displayed the same tartan pattern as Calum's kilt. I sat as still as I could, watching her. She moved with purpose but also grace.

I do not know how long I had been staring at her when she turned around and saw me. Embarrassed, I looked down at the blankets. It was the first time I noticed that the other bed had no blanket on it and I had two. Calum must have given me his when he left.

"Morning, lassie," the woman said. Her voice was soft, smooth, and kind. Taken aback by her demeanor, I could not find my tongue. "It's alright. You've been through quite an ordeal. It may take some time to set things straight in your mind. My name is Anna."

A name as beautiful as she.

"Hello, ma'am," I managed.

"Anna," she corrected.

"Anna." I repeated, grateful for the gesture. She seemed older than me but not by too much, five or six years, maybe. My manners took over and I was able to introduce myself and give her my name.

"Aye, Mercy," Anna said as she began to fuss around the small space, poking the fire and setting a small cauldron and pan on it. "Calum told us. He also told us of your terrible journey and the mission you still have ahead of you."

My, Calum had been busy. Why did he find it necessary to talk about my business with everyone in the village before I even had a chance to wake? Anna knowing the dire circumstances in which I found myself increased my discomfort.

"Once Calum told the chief the details of your mission and your deadline, John sent a few scouts out to see if they could locate Henderson. It should not be any more than a week or so."

"Excuse me. Who is Henderson?"

"The seannachie. The man who may know of this other man you seek."

I flung off the covers and leapt to my feet.

"He is coming back? Now?"

Anna straightened up for a moment at my sudden movement. "Calm yourself, lassie. John sent for him but the scouts have to find him first. It could still take days."

Or weeks, I thought. I sat on the edge of the bed. From hope to dashed hopes as quick as a blink.

"Do not fret lass," Anna said as she rubbed her hands in her apron. "There is plenty to do while you wait for his return. Starting with getting you a proper meal and tending to your clothes."

I looked down at myself. I truly looked a fright. Burrs stuck up and down my stockings, there were at least three sizable tears in my outer skirts, and the ends of my sleeves were near black with filth. I tried to diminish the sight of the damage by putting my hands behind my back. I had no desire to see the horrid state of my hair after all those days without wearing a proper bonnet.

"No need to feel poorly about it," Anna said turning back to the fire. "We are all a little worn after a journey. There's some ham heating in the pan. Calum should be in soon with some eggs and some sort of baked goodie, if he can charm one of the ladies." She chuckled a bit before completing her thought. "He certainly has come into his own in that respect. What a little charmer."

Calum? Really? If Calum is what passed for charming in this village, it was going to be a dull and difficult stay. No matter, I was here for information not to be charmed or entertained.

Many odors and scents fought for dominance in the small space. There were dirt, dust and general muck smells, with animal smells being particularly strong. It was strange but I thought I smelled a few herbs and maybe lavender? It had to be my imagination as plants do not grow indoors and it seemed unlikely that plants from outside could compete with the indoor odors. The one scent that seemed to thread its way through them all was the sweet smell of frying ham. Mmmm. The thought of eating helped me find my tongue again.

"It certainly has been a tiresome journey. I would much appreciate the chance to scrub these clothes, not to mention my face," I said. Remembering my manners once again I added another thought. "Thank you, Anna, for your kindness."

"No need for thanks," she replied as she removed the small cauldron from the fire with an iron hook and placed it on the small hearth in front of the fire. She grabbed it by the handle with cloth dampers and poured a bit into a shallow bowl on the table that separated the sleeping area where I still stood and the working area near the fire. Anna reached up, causing me to follow her hands with my eyes. She pulled a few stalks from a bundle of lavender hanging above me and dropped it in the hot water. Lavender. It was the first time I noticed the bundles of plants hanging upside down from the rafter above the table.

"For your face and hands," Anna said, then handed me a small swatch of cloth. "Give it a minute or you'll burn your hands. Dry off with this."

"Aye," I said. Uncertain whether I should thank her again or not. I decided to study the plants instead. The herbs I had smelled were indeed real. Overhead there were about a dozen bunches of herbs and plants, most of which I recognized. There were cooking herbs like sage, thyme, something that looked like thistle, and wild garlic but few for healing. I recognized heather, meadowsweet, and spearmint, but not any others. This woman was a cook, not a healer.

"Anna?" I asked. She had already turned back to the fire, busy with her next set of chores. "Are you related to Calum?"

"We're all related in the glen, dear."

"Yes, um, aye. You are members of the same clan. I meant to ask if you are his sister or aunt or kin of some nature."

"Blood kin? Not the kind you mean. We all shared enough spilt blood to be kin."

"Of course, ma'am. I mean no offense. I was curious how we came to stay with you, here, last night."

"I had room."

She had room. Simple as that. It was not that it was her turn or that she shared a kinship or felt a certain special connection to Calum. She simply had room.

"And it's Anna," she said with a mild, scolding tone. "Go on, now. Before the water cools too much."

Chapter Twenty Eight

After I cleaned my face and hands and tucked under the filthiest parts of my sleeves until I could properly scrub them, I felt a bit better. Anna lifted the ham out of the pan and cut it into three equal pieces. She had probably planned to feast on the piece of ham by herself before we arrived. My stomach tightened with guilt.

This first portion of our meal smelled delicious. The guilt over taking some of Anna's food was not strong enough to keep me from eating. Calum arrived as Anna and I were finishing our ham. He carried three eggs and two pastries.

"They are large enough to share," he said, motioning to the scones. These were the first words he had spoken to me since arriving in his glen.

"Did the Hendersons see you?" Anna asked as he set everything on the table in front of Anna.

"Nae," he said. "I was quiet enough."

"Wait, the Hendersons?" I asked. "Are you saying the storyteller is back?"

"The Hendersons are the sons of Henderson, the seannachie," Anna explained. "They can be quite awful."

I wondered what that meant as Anna expertly cracked the eggs into the still hot pan. Calum grabbed the ham set aside for him and ate it standing up. We all watched the flames turn the non-yellow parts of the eggs from clear and runny to white and spongy. It was easier than trying to think of what to say to one another.

"Where did you get the scones?"

"Mary MacWaters. I said I would rake out her hearth later. She would have given me more but this was all she had."

I tried to wrap my head around the idea of how the clan worked. They were intertwined in some ways, yet divided in others. Calum mentioned doing some sort of trade for the scones but not for the eggs. Why? Clearly Anna had her own animals. Was that how it was for everyone? Were there communal animals as well, like perhaps the chickens? Then why did he fear the Hendersons knowing he had gotten us eggs?

One thing I did understand about the glen was everyone had a part to play, a reason the other clan members wanted them here. I knew I needed to find a way to make myself useful while we waited for the return of the storyteller, whose name was also Henderson. It seemed my knowledge of herbs would be helpful, and hopefully wanted, but I would also be required to do manual chores, something with which I did not have much experience. I most certainly did not want to be asked to do any spying or "scouting" as they called it.

Anna sprinkled some dried herb over the eggs before we ate. My egg tasted even more marvelous than the ham. Calum sat down for the occasion. He insisted, above Anna's objections, that she enjoy one of the scones in full. The half scone I shared with Calum was dry but sweeter than I expected. I wondered how the baker had managed it.

It occurred to me after a few minutes that no one was speaking. I had become used to Calum's habit to stay quiet but Anna who had been quite talkative while we were alone had fallen silent. She and Calum were not looking at each other. Was Calum embarrassed for leaving? Was Anna ashamed of him, shunning him? That seemed unlikely as she had been lovely to me. Of course, Calum said people in the glen were fiercely proud of being generous to strangers and visitors. She had allowed us both to stay with her. Would she allow us to stay for as long as it took to see the seannachie? Would we be passed from home to home? Would we stay together? Why did the thought that we would not bother me?

The silence stretched on as we ate. I glanced over at Calum and saw little raised red bumps on his arm. Midge bites. I rose from the bench we shared and pulled down some lavender from the same bundle Anna had used for my washing bowl. I placed it between my palms and rubbed them slowly back and forth, allowing the flecks of lavender to fall to the table. The scent was delightful as it mixed with the lingering smells from our meal. Then I added a few crumbs from the scone and a tiny bit of water, combining it all to make a paste. I steadied Calum's arm, impressed that he did not retract at my touch, and smeared the salve on the area of his skin with the most bites.

"If only you could find a way to prevent them from biting in the first place," he mumbled.

"You are welcome."

Anna smiled at my response.

"You could wear the poultice," Anna said to Calum, the first words I heard them exchange.

Calum looked at Anna for a moment but said nothing in reply.

"Are you saying there is something that will keep them from biting? Is that why they are not in the house with us now?"

"They never come inside," Calum mumbled, staring at the last bite of his scone before popping it in his mouth.

Anna gave him a sidewise glance. "That is true, the little creatures never come indoors but as soon as you go outside, they attack, often in huge groups."

"Yes, we saw swarms on our journey. You mentioned a poultice? Is there something that keeps them from biting?"

"If you wear a cloth soaked in warm lavender water, it keeps the vile creatures from getting too close. It's funny to think that something that is so pleasant to us repels them."

"Why does everyone not do that?" I asked with true sincerity.

"It doesn't work for everyone," Calum said. "Besides a warm cloth around my neck dripping liquid down my back is irritating."

"As are midge bites," Anna replied.

Calum shifted in his seat. He placed his hand on his side for a moment and I thought I saw the slightest wince.

"With all of your bundles," I said as I pointed above where we sat, "do you have lemongrass?"

"I donnae clip lemongrass. Never had a need for it." Anna stood as she spoke. I followed her lead. The meal over, it was time for chores. We could discuss lemongrass while scrubbing the morning dishes.

"You can interrogate Anna about her plants later," Calum said.

"I thank you for all that you have done for me, Anna," I added.

"Go on. See what John has planned for you."

Anna turned her back to us, waved a hand in our general direction, and continued her chores. It surprised me. I thought she would at least smile.

Chapter Twenty Nine

"You embarrassed her," Calum said as soon as we were out the door. I was sure Anna could still hear us.

"I meant no such thing. I simply wanted her to know that I was grateful."

"You have much to learn about the glen."

No argument from me. This place had as many rules and secrets as a royal palace. Not that I had ever been to one or knew anyone who had ever been to one but I had overheard plenty of stories from Uncle's visitors. Those men gossiped more than the washer-women.

"John will have had the night to determine what will happen," Calum explained, as if I could not figure that out on my own. My resentment at his treatment grew stronger but I held my tongue. I was in enough trouble without alienating the only people who had a chance of helping me fulfill my mission.

"Anna said she thought MacIain would send scouts looking for Mr. Henderson," I ventured. "Do you think he will?"

"It is one possibility," Calum said, "but not the only one. Quiet, John's bothie is over there."

Glencoe was an enormous area with majestic views and breath-taking sights but the village was small. There were houses, bothies as Calum called them, as well as common areas with animal pens, a large fire pit and paths that snaked out in different directions. I assumed at least one went to a water source, like a river. It was so different from my area of London. Here there were no carriages in the streets, no constant noises from people shouting, metal clanging, and the slam-ming of wooden crates being stacked and unstacked in alleys. The glen was much quieter but by no means idle. Folks indoors and out were busy with their own bustling, getting chores done, preparing for the day. Somehow, they managed to do so with more pleasant sounds.

When we arrived at MacIain's door, Calum cleared his throat. A voice from inside, presumably MacIain's, told us to enter.

"Sir," Calum said once we were inside. He nodded to his chief who was alone in his quarters. I had expected to see Leith as well but MacIain sat alone at a table covered in papers, food scraps and four candles. It was quite dark in the small abode.

"Good greetings, sir," I said. It felt awkward even as it came out of my mouth but it is what I would have said to someone of MacIain's status if I had met him in London.

"Aye," he replied, glancing at us before returning his eyes to the papers before him. "I see you both survived a night in a proper bed." For a moment I thought he had implied that we had spent the night in the same bed and quickly opened my mouth to correct him. Calum shot me one of the glances he used when he wanted to keep me from speaking. Anna had been witness to the innocence of our sleeping arrangement and I felt confident I could call on her testimony if needed.

"Aye, sir," Calum responded. "Anna was kind enough to give Mercy and me her spare bunks." Was it my imagination or did he draw out the "s" sound to emphasis that there had been separate beds?

"Right," MacIain replied, clearly moving on to other things in his mind. He lifted his head and looked straight at me with his powerful blue eyes. "You may stay with her until we hear from Henderson, if you wish." I nodded to indicate that I would. "Right. You are not a prisoner, Mercy, but as long as you choose to stay, you will be expected to contribute to the clan."

"Aye, sir," I said, before Calum could try to answer for me. "I am good with plants and herbs for easing ailments."

"She is, sir," Calum offered, even though the chief had not challenged the notion. "She made a paste this morning for my midge bites and I donnae feel the itch now. Plus, she picks these special daisies that cure headaches."

"No doubt a helpful talent," MacIain looked as if he were going to ask me something and then stopped and returned his eyes to his papers. "We will try to remember what you teach us so we can use it after you leave."

"Aye, sir." It was getting easier to say 'aye.' "I can also cook some, scrub pots and pans, and sew about anything although I am better at weaving."

"Weaving?" MacIain asked without looking at me.

"Aye, sir," I said, feeling uncomfortable for the first time during the conversation. Why had I volunteered that information? "I am told my mother was an excellent weaver."

"You do not know your mother?"

Sharing the details of my life was not something I was used to doing or liked in the least. Unfortunately, the only path to fulfilling my mission was through John. He had to know everything that I did in order to help.

"No, sir. They died. That is, my parents died when I was a baby. I was sent to live with my uncle, my mother's brother, in London. He did not like to talk about them. When I was old enough to weave, he told me about my mother's talent but then stopped talking about them all together. Is that important, sir?"

"Perhaps yes, perhaps not." We were all silent for a while, the only sounds were the papers shuffling as MacIain rearranged them and guttural sounds from the cattle in the bothie.

"Sir," I ventured, "does this mean you've decided to help me?"

"Aye, well, we will try to assist you in your quest," MacIain said.

Some part of me thought I would feel a surge of joy or hopefulness at his offer but instead I felt something else. Sadness? Emptiness? A sense of dread at having another group of people to let down if I ultimately failed?

Calum poked me in the side with his elbow and I realized I had not responded.

"Uh, thank you, sir," I said. I was allowed to thank the chief but not my hostess? How would I survive in this place?

"Donnae thank me, yet," he said. I wanted to nudge Calum back but resisted the urge. "The lads went out at first light. I'll let you know as soon I hear anything."

"Thank you for trying, sir." It was all I could think to say.

MacIain waved his hand in the air in a similar gesture to the one Anna had used as we had left her earlier. This time, I took it to mean we had been dismissed.

Chapter Thirty

I spent the rest of the day with Anna, doing what she called 'properly preparing' for our stay with her. Calum disappeared after mumbling something about seeing to his own chores. It seemed, at least for the moment, Calum and I would remain in Anna's home together.

"No time for a full brushing now, but we can minimize further dirt by getting your hair into braids," Anna suggested.

I sat on a stool in the bothie and tried to hold in tears as Anna pulled and separated my hair in an attempt to control it. With so many days out of a bonnet, it was matted with dirt, dried mud, muck of all kinds and was likely home to more than one insect. The pain was so bad, I almost asked her to stop. Eventually, she managed to get my hair into two braids, one on each side of my head. It felt nice to wear weaves. I pretended it would make my mom happy.

"Once we give it a good brushing, we can get it into one large braid." I noticed that Anna's bun was actually one long braid pulled into a tight circle.

"Aye. That would be nice. This is good for now." I did not say 'thank you' as it seemed to make these Highlanders uncomfortable.

With my new braids in place, Anna and I got to work on the both-ie. We hauled lengths of all types of cloth, from plaids to flax sheets to thick swaths which laid on the ground inside, hung them over large boulders nearby and beat the dust out of them with a broom. It was strangely satisfying to whack the sheets and rugs as hard as I could. Not because of the dirt and dust flying out of them, rendering them cleaner, but because it felt good to let out a little anger. Anna was a wise woman.

Calum returned late-afternoon, as Anna pulled a meat pie off the hot coals on the hearth. He did not speak while we ate. When the meal was finished, I stood up to gather the plates for washing.

"Wait a minute, Mercy," he said. His voice was low and he did not look at me when he spoke. I knew this could not be good news.

"Has MacIain called the scouts back, already?" I asked, panic closing in on me.

"No," Calum said, "nothing like that." I relaxed a bit but still braced for whatever he was about to say.

"I'd been doing the calculations and confirmed it with John. Today is June first." He paused to let the meaning of that sink in before stating it out loud. "Which means we have twenty-one days to figure out where you are supposed to meet Mr. Kingsnot Silver, get there, and find him. With no idea how far a journey that will be, you must be prepared to go at any time."

"Is there not enough in the journey pack from the MacGregors?"

"There is no way to know until we have a destination but that is not what I was thinking."

He put his hand in the folds of his cloak and I thought for a moment he was adjusting for his wound. Instead, he pulled out paper and a quill.

"With Anna's help, we can make you some ink. John said you can use the backs of these papers that are out of date and not useful anymore."

I understood what he meant. I needed to remember the poem now when my mind was calm, at least compared to while we were traveling.

"The poem," I said in a soft voice.

"What poem?" Anna asked.

I was hesitant to tell anyone else about this part of the plan but it was clear that Calum had told at least John if not others. Plus we had been talking about it in front of Anna in her home so I told her about the importance of the poem and how I lost it.

"And the poem is the one way to get this man to believe you are the person he is waiting for?" she asked after I explained it.

"Yes, aye," I said. "Mr. Silver will not believe me if I do not know the poem."

"Then we better get started," Anna said.

It turned into a long and difficult night. We were still exhausted from our journey and adjusting to Glencoe. My body wanted rest but my heart knew I had to get the poem right to fulfill my duty and to learn about my family. It had been dark for many hours by the time I was satisfied that I had it all. Calum put the paper in front of me and asked me to read it again to be sure that I had it right. Then he told me to memorize it again. He wanted to hide the paper in Anna's home so it would not be stolen again.

Calum's sincere efforts to help me finish my mission made me both happy and sad. I was happy to have his help and sad that he felt obligated to give it. His sense of honor and duty appeared to be limitless, no matter the issue at hand.

That night, Anna fell asleep quickly while Calum and I lay in our individual beds and talked. Well, I talked and Calum tried not to.

"How has everyone been treating you?" I asked.

"Fine."

"Fine," I repeated. "Have they asked why you came back?"

"They know. You."

I wanted to ask if that was the only reason but did not.

"How do you feel being here?"

"Tired." With that he rolled over and I heard snoring a few moments later. I doubted he was asleep.

Chapter Thirty One

At first I was concerned about how the other clan members would react to me. It turned out there was little acknowledgement of my arrival at all. In a small village, my name and reason for being there were probably known by all before I woke that first morning and met Anna. When we came across a person I had not met, they did not stop to introduce themselves nor was I introduced to them. They simply nodded and said my name as they did with Anna. She would whisper their names to me a little while later. Strange. I wondered if it was because they knew I would not be staying or if this was how newcomers were always treated. It was not rude exactly but it was not welcoming, either.

The days we spent in the glen passed pleasantly enough. Anna and I planted vegetables, weeded the plant beds, milked cows, gathered eggs, prepared meals, darned and mended clothing, beat the rugs, baked with Mary MacWaters, and attended scripture readings and evening fires. My personal chore was going on long outings alone or with Calum to gather plants and herbs. Later, Anna and I would sort them, bundle them and decide which ones to dry. Throughout it all, I recited the poem, trying to figure out if I had it right, exactly right.

"I followed a peacock to some hyssop this morning," I said to Calum one evening. "It was growing out of the rock wall by Mary's place. It is a wonderful, useful plant."

"A peacock?" Calum asked. "Are you sure you're feeling okay?"

"It is the common name of a butterfly," I said, fighting the urge to roll my eyes.

"Right. Why do I need to know that?" he asked.

"What you need to know is that I found hyssop. Let me check your wound," I begged. "I am certain the hyssop can help."

"Nae. It's fine. Leave me be, lassie!" Calum replied while rewrapping the upper portion of his kilt around his shoulder. He winced as he did so and tried to hide it from me.

"You should let her take a look," Anna urged. "Mercy is quite a fine healer."

I had been there less than seven days and already people were coming to me for advice on how to treat their minor ailments. Glencoe was a marvelous place for a healer. The fields held many useful plants, especially clusters of foxglove with tortoiseshell and blue butterflies reaching in the long blossoms for nectar. Foxglove ointments healed scabs fast.

Contributing to the health of the clan made me happy. I wished the two people to whom I owed the most, MacIain and Calum, would take my advice. Even Anna used the new midge repellant. A simple weave of two parts lemon grass and one part lavender worn around the neck, wrist or ankle proved an excellent remedy for some. There were others who did not see any advantage to it. Everyone is different.

"I know she is a good healer," he said. "My head always aches less after eating the daisies and little Margaret's stomach no longer pains her after Mercy gave her tea from the plant near the river's marshy area. Even Matthew Robinson's back is strong enough to carry firewood after the compress she made for him."

"Fine. Now let me take a look at that wound."

"Nae! I have work to do." His last words were not out of his mouth before his body was through the door.

Anna gave me a small smile. "Do not fret. He'll come around." She returned to her work while I was left to wonder what she meant.

There were many questions about Anna I did not dare ask. Where was her family? Had they died in the massacre? How had she rebuilt her home while others were still unfinished? Why had she treated Calum so coldly at first and yet nice now?

It was a curious thing, the way the people of Glencoe treated Calum. Every day he got up before the sun and was usually out until after it went down, coming in only for the morning and evening meals. There were plenty of projects going on in the village. Loads of building and mending of things previously built. There were days when he did not come in for meals.

"Where do you suppose Calum is today?" I asked Anna after we had cleaned up our morning meal and were sewing patches on the holes in my skirts. We had determined there was too much fabric lost to simply stitch the holes shut. Anna had found some scraps to use from an old plaid of hers.

"With the scouts, I assume," Anna said while scrunching up her face as she studied the next section we had to patch. "That or cattle-rustling." She said it so matter-of-factly that I had to process for a moment she had actually said it.

"Cattle-rustling?" I asked.

"Aye," she replied. "He's been working hard to gain the respect of the others."

"Why should he need to do that?" I asked. "Calum believes he should have done more?" I wanted to hear what she thought about the massacre and those who survived. After all, she survived, did she not?

"When Calum was young, well younger, the Henderson's used to tease him something awful as they did everyone smaller than themselves. On that day, that vicious, despicable day, Calum's sense of honor was severely wounded. Honor wounds are slow to heal. If they do at all."

As I thought about Calum and his honor, I watched Anna, apparently having made her decision on what to patch, set to work on the worst section of the skirt. We worked with her comments sitting in the air between us, the only sound was the fire crackling even though the afternoon sun had warmed the village.

"Let's sit outside to sew," Anna said. "It's the first nice day in a while, at least until the rains begin again."

I had been in Scotland less than a month and I was already used to the random waves of weather that rolled through. If it was sunny, rain, hail, ice or snow could suddenly fall from the sky and last minutes or days. If it was raining, there were strange stretches of time when it would stop, then start again some time later. There was something charming about it. Also, something annoying. London had sudden rainstorms, too, but somehow in Scotland it fit the personalities of the people as well. Somewhat charming, somewhat frustrating.

"Your uncle must miss you something terrible," Anna said once we were settled outside, she on a rock and me on the ground.

"My uncle waits for me as a farmer waits for his cow. Or as he waits for the silverware to be set. He is not a man given to emotions."

"Everyone has emotions," Anna said. "Perhaps he is not apt at expressing them."

"Aye, everyone has them," I replied. "Not everyone chooses to be affected by them."

Without looking at me, missing a stitch or raising her voice in the slightest, Anna managed to hand out the biggest reprimand of my life. A scolding for which there was no possible response.

"Perhaps then, you should comfort yourself with having a single family member that has not been slaughtered in his own bed by an enemy under trust."

Chapter Thirty Two

Thirteen days. I was in Glencoe for thirteen days before there was any word about Henderson, the seannachie. I had become used to the rhythms of the glen and the people, too. Once they knew and trusted someone, they were downright warm.

We were gathered at an evening fire. Linus, one of the older men in the group, had been telling a wonderful tale about a woman warrior in a place called Skye. He was interrupted when two men appeared from the shadows and reported to their chief. I marveled at how the scouts could sneak up on the group in spite of the strong stench of sweat and animals they carried.

Every time a scout came to camp, my heart beat faster and my stomach tensed. There had never been a message for me until that night.

"Mercy." MacIain said.

I stood when the chief addressed me. I had not been told to do so but everyone else did so I thought it the proper thing to do.

"Henderson has been found and told to return," MacIain reported. "He is three days out."

I regretted my choice to stand as my legs wobbled at the news. Excitement shot through me as I learned he had been located and dread soon followed upon learning he was not minutes away but days.

"Aye, sir," I said. "Can I set out to meet him?"

"No."

No? Why not? Why was MacIain making me wait even longer than necessary? If the scouts knew he was three days out, then they knew where he was and could tell me. I felt Calum's hand grab mine and give a gentle tug. My time with the chief was up, at least for the moment. I did not hear a single word that was spoken during the rest of time we sat by the fire.

"Why can I not go?" I spat at Calum as soon as we were far enough away from everyone else on the path to Anna's. Calum did not follow the path, he kept walking toward the fields and I stayed right beside him. I planned to keep walking until I found Henderson or Mr. Silver.

"Think it through, Mercy," he said. "You're letting your emotions block your mind from the simple truth. If the seannachie knows anything or knows nothing, you have no idea in what direction you will have to travel. Going out to meet him could cost you time in your next step. Letting him come to you is the best you can do."

"Why did the scouts not ask him about Mr. Silver? I could have my answer and be on my way!"

Calum stopped walking. He grabbed me by my shoulders and forced me to look at him.

"Mercy." The calmness of his voice surprised me. "Think. You have to know that the scouts are a series of people throughout the hills, mountains, valleys, glens, marshes, and plains. They are experts at staying hidden or hiding in plain sight when they eavesdrop or confronting someone directly or whatever the situation warrants. But they're also experts in communicating without words. They leave signs, cuts in tree bark, dropped messages, cloth tied in a particular spot. Relaying something this complicated without a pre-arranged signal would be useless. Whatever arrived at the glen would be as distorted as gossip from Edinburgh."

The fact that he was absolutely correct did not ease my frustration.

"You use the word 'scouts' but you mean 'spies.' These men lurking in the wilderness passing signals as messages are all spies!"

"Aye, yeah. Pretty good ones, too. Some of the best in Scotland. But they cannae tell you what they donnae know. They did tell you that Henderson knows he is needed in the glen by the chief. He will be here as fast as he can."

Calum dropped his grasp on my shoulders and turned in the direction of the largest mountain. I was breathing heavy, both from our walk and from the anger that flooded my body. He was still, staring straight forward. It was dark but we were far enough from the fire that my eyes adjusted to see the faint outline of the mountain ridges. We stood for a long time with only the sounds of the night creatures. Eventually my breathing slowed. I knew Calum was right, I had no choice but to stay in Glencoe until Henderson could get here. A maddening proposition.

"Dragons," Calum whispered.

"Did you say 'dragons' just then?" I asked. I had been lost in my own thoughts when he spoke.

"Aye. Dory and Gilbert called the mountains sleeping dragons because of how the ridges look at dusk, dawn, and in the fog. Like dragons curled up on their bellies."

I knew a bit about who Dory was but had not heard Gilbert's name before. I had met everyone in the glen which meant he likely had been murdered in the massacre. I decided not to press Calum on it.

"They do look a bit like dragons," I offered. "Do they have names?"

"The dragons?"

"The mountains."

"Of course they have names. That big one, the one that saved so many MacDonalds that horrible morning is Meall Mor. Those who were able to hike to the other side of it found shelter and protection in the woods. The murdering cowards did not follow."

I expected more emotion from Calum. I had expected to have a conversation like this while we were in the glen. I was surprised it took him so long to do it. Why wasn't he crying, shaking a fist in anger, sputtering out his words? Why did he sound calm all the time? I knew he cared deeply for people and about honor. How did he manage to hide his emotions? Why did he?

"That sounds like a nice name, Meall Mor. What does it mean?"

Calum did not answer. Instead he stood, still and staring. It occurred to me that he may have wanted to be alone with his memories of that horrible time. I backed up a few steps, then turned in the direction of the village and Anna's bothie which I realized I now thought of as home. My heart ached for Calum and all that he was going through being back in Glencoe with the memories of his family and clansmen being slaughtered in front of him. Tears formed in my eyes as I walked and I did not try to keep them from falling.

"Big mound."

I turned to see Calum had caught up with me. He could move in absolute silence. I guess that made sense seeing as he was a spy.

"What?" I asked.

"Meall Mor. It means Big Mound." He gave a sort of half smile. I smiled back.

Clever.

Chapter Thirty Three

T hose three days were impossibly long. On the second day we had a terrible rain storm. Stuck inside for hours, there was little to do but weave, cook, and fret about how the weather could be slowing Henderson's progress.

"It's not an exact number," Calum reminded me. "The trip could take a little longer."

"I know," I said. "That is what worries me so. I am rapidly running out of days. What if he cannot help?"

Calum was silent again. We both knew there was no way to answer my question.

I was up before the sun on the third day. Not before Calum, though. His bunk held nothing but a thin blanket. Anna and I pulled all the plant bundles down from the rafters and laid them on the table to see what she had.

"Since we were stuck in here yesterday, I thought it would be good to spend the day outdoors searching for more plants to bundle. With all that rain, and the warm sun today, there should be plenty in bloom to gather."

The sun was shining and all the creatures in the glen were scurrying about gathering food and enjoying the good weather while they could. Anna talked on about the pleasant weather of early summer and how it was the best time to locate some of her most useful plants but I knew the truth of our task that day. She wanted to keep me busy with something that I liked, away from the village, to try to keep my mind off Henderson's arrival. What a lovely lady.

"I know he may not arrive today," I said.

"Who?" she asked.

I looked at her out of the corner of my eye and smiled. "I am happy to spend the day in the fields. I hope it is not the whole day."

"Trust is tricky, Mercy," she said. "Try to trust that you will get what you need soon."

I did not have to wait the whole day. Anna and I had surveyed her bundles and talked about what we needed. Then we grabbed out cloth carriers and headed outside. Anna walked right into Calum as he was coming in the door. They stumbled together for a moment then Calum looked past her to me.

"The scouts say he will be here within the hour."

Pacing is not a good use of time but it was all I could manage. My mind would not stay on one task long enough to accomplish anything. What if he did not know Mr. Silver? What if he did but I did not have enough time to get there? What if Henderson demanded a trade for his knowledge? What if? What if? What if?

"Say your poem," Calum called to me.

I performed my useless pacing outside MacIain's bothie because that was where Henderson would need to report. MacIain was not inside, of course. He had plenty of clan business that required his attention elsewhere.

"Right, the poem," I replied. I tried but my mind was too full of 'what if' questions.

"Here!" the call went up throughout the village. Henderson had arrived.

The next ten to twenty minutes were excruciating. Henderson, an average sized man wearing a kilt of another clan, arrived and was immediately given food and drink. MacIain was found and returned home to greet his clansman. The two entered the chief's bothie. A crowd gathered outside where Calum and I stood as the people of Glencoe found time to put off their daily chores to wait around in the middle of the day. Even the Henderson lads joined us, presumably to see their father. MacIain and Henderson held a private conversation that lasted far too long in my opinion. Finally, finally, MacIain called for Calum and me to join them inside. Many of the villagers followed us.

"Calum!" Henderson said and stood from his perch near the fire. "I was about to say good to see you lad but you are no longer a lad!"

"Aye, sir." Strangely, Calum showed no emotion at seeing this man. "This is Mercy. Did John tell you why she's here?"

"Aye, he did. I'm afraid I do not have good news." He turned to look at me. "Lass, tell me the name of the man you need to meet again?"

I cleared my throat to be sure he heard me. He had already said he did not have good news and my tongue felt numb from fear. "Mr. Kingsnot Silver."

Henderson stood quiet for a while. "I am not aware of any man with that name or anything close to it. Could it be some sort of coded message?"

Of course the spies think everything is a code.

"Is there any more to what your uncle told you about the message?" Henderson asked.

"No, sir. I only know that I am to give the message to a Mr. Kingsnot Silver."

"*Kingsnot* Silver. Kingsnot *Silver*..." Henderson repeated it over and over and over at different cadences as if trying to spark a memory.

Tears rolled down my face. I did not sob or make a sound. I felt Calum lay a hand on my shoulder in an offer of compassion for my loss. He had no idea how much had been lost. Now that I could not deliver the message, the results would impact not only me but everyone protected under the Alliance. Including Calum.

Plus, I would never know anything more about my family history.

"Kingsnot *Silver*. King*snot* Silver. *King*snot Silver." The expression on the storyteller's face changed to a wry smile.

"Is it possible he said Stirling, not Silver?" Henderson asked.

I looked up at him. "Sterling Silver?" I asked.

"When you heard 'Stirling' you thought of sterling silver, the kind used in fancy candlesticks and tableware? You substituted 'silver' for 'sterling.' Sterling silver is with an "e" while the Scottish town of Stirling has an 'i'," he paused for a moment before finishing. "Kingsnot isn't one word, it's two words: King's Knot."

Chapter Thirty Four

Calum's face paled a bit. The Hendersons nudged each other and some of the adults whispered to one another while others smiled. They all understood what the storyteller had figured out but I did not.

"You know of someone in a town called Stirling?" Excitement shot through me. Could this be the information I needed?

"It is your formality that tricked you," the seannachie said. "Drop the word 'mister' and it is no longer a person. It's a place. He told you to go to King's Knot at Stirling,"

I stared at him with confusion. This seemed a great revelation to the gathered clanspeople. There was a collective snort of comprehension as they grinned at each other and murmured but the meaning of what he was saying eluded me.

"Lass, there is a garden at Stirling Castle called the King's Knot. 'Knot' as in tied rope. The King's Knot at Stirling Castle. That is where you need to go."

Calum and I both stared at Henderson, unable to speak.

"Midsummer at Stirling, just like the Bruce!" one of the Henderson lads said to no one in particular. His brother punched him in the shoulder.

There was room in my head for one thought. We wasted so much time! If I had not assumed that my uncle was saying a person's name and had remembered Stirling, not silver, I could have told Calum where I needed to go from the moment he found me at the coach crash. All that time, all that we endured was a waste. I could have completed my task by now. The enormity of my blunder was difficult to grasp.

"Whatever it is that you need to do is in Stirling," Henderson offered. "That's eighty miles or so from here."

Calum had still not regained the ability to speak. His mind must have been having trouble with all of this as well.

I had only four days until midsummer.

"Thank you. Thank you for understanding my uncle's instructions. I wish I could stay to pay you back but I have to start out immediately if Calum and I are going to reach it by midsummer."

The seannachie looked at MacIain and then to Anna. It was Anna who spoke.

"Lassie. You won't get there in time. The two of you cannae make your way through the Trossachs around to Stirling by midsummer's midnight."

"We have to," I insisted, logic and geography had no place in my mind. "I have to deliver the message. I cannot fail my family."

The seannachie stepped closer and took my small hand in his enormous one. The softness of his palm surprised me as I expected his whole hand, not only his fingertips to be calloused. He took my hand and held it up to his chin. Without thinking, my eyes followed and soon I was staring him in the face.

"You cannae make it."

"Not if I stand around gabbing with you all day." I pulled my hand down hard in order to escape his grasp and headed back to Anna's to gather my things.

Everyone followed me the short distance and stood outside, peering through the small window. No one spoke as I gathered the travel sack from the MacGregors, restocked by Anna the night before and stuffed with treasures I had gained whilst among these Highlanders. I had already packed my clothing, now patched and bearing marks of the Glencoe tartan that I had come to think of as my own. When I grabbed for my canteen, another hand reached out to stop me. This was not the soft-palmed hand of the seannachie but a fully calloused hand with scars.

Calum.

"Henderson is right," he said. "We cannae make it."

Gutted. The only single word to address the feeling I had at that moment. Pain, disappointment, embarrassment, fear, frustration, uncertainty, mixed with more feelings for which I had no words. Gutted.

My shoulders drooped and I looked at the ceiling to avoid seeing Calum. I had failed in the most complete sense of the word. I had not accomplished my mission. The Alliance would falter if not outright fail and I would never know about my family. All because I misunderstood Kingsnot to be a name of a man and assumed Stirling, like sterling, referred to silver. To make things even worse, I had dragged Calum through it all.

I dropped my head, trying to hide the tears now streaming down my cheeks. I could feel everyone staring at me, unsure what to say. What could they say to the clan-less lass who mixed up silver and Stirling? Before I could fall to the ground in a full out sob, I heard Calum speak.

"But I can."

Chapter Thirty Five

"What?" I asked, picking up my chin to look Calum in the eyes. "What do you mean *you* can make it?"

"Henderson and Anna are correct. The two of us would not be able to navigate the countryside between here and Stirling by midsummer. But I can do it alone. I know the Trossachs well enough to travel them blindfolded, I am an expert at not being seen unless I want to be and when I have to be out in the open, a Scottish lad traveling alone is much less unusual than one accompanied by a girl from London."

"Calum is right, Mercy," MacIain said. "The skills he honed during his time with Red Rob will serve him well on this journey."

"Calum's not interesting enough to catch anyone's attention," Ian Henderson said. "He'll make it there easy."

A few more people spoke up, assuring me that Calum would be able to take my quest to its rightful end. It pained me to hear how heartfelt they were in their desire to ease my fears whilst I knew that it was not possible for anyone, not even Calum, to rescue me. I had to complete my task myself.

"Nae," I said loud enough for all who were talking to hear. "It is not possible. I have to be the one that makes the trip."

"Mercy," Calum protested, "I can do it alone but we will not make it in time if we go together. Go over the message you memorized with me and I'll set out within a quarter hour."

I looked at Calum, earnest in his generous offer to help. I glanced at the others who thought this was the best course of action. Unfortunately, I knew one thing they did not. I knew the truth.

"Nae," I repeated. This time with a certain snap to the word. "Repeating the poem is only the first step. The message is not in words. It's a tapestry, one which I have been learning since I was old enough to hold a bobbin. I cannot tell you the message. I must be there to create it."

The people who had gathered around us fidgeted and rustled a bit but no one spoke. They all looked to Calum, as if my fate were up to him. He looked at me with concern, confusion and perhaps pride all at once.

"Right, then. Let's get started."

Calum grabbed his own packed rucksack He had already tied a bedroll across the bottom. Perhaps he feared I would leave camp without him if he did not hurry. Few minutes passed between Calum's declaration that we would leave and the moment of leaving. I needed to get on the road if we had any chance of making it to Stirling in time but found my feet were not itching to get moving.

All those weeks ago when I pulled out of London, done up in a nice dress with my hair twisted into a neat bun tucked under a fancy bonnet, I had bid the house servants a quick goodbye, climbed into the carriage with my chaperone and rode away. My uncle was not even home at the time. Leaving Glencoe was quite different. Everyone continued to ignore their chores and gathered around us. I wore the same dress, altered and showing evidence of my time in the Highlands. Different, too, was my hair, now braided. Anna had been right that it was better for chores and traveling.

No one seemed to know how big a goodbye to say to Calum. Was this a quick journey, simply to help me deliver my message? Would he come back here or go back to MacGregor and his men? MacIain spoke to him privately, then clapped him on the shoulder with one hand and shook hands with him with the other. Some of the Glencoe men shook Calum's hand and most of the women waved. Many people shouted encouragements for the journey. It seemed they appreciated all the work he had done for them.

My goodbyes were easier to label but not easier to say. They were forever goodbyes. The clan had not known me long but we all knew that I would not be coming back. Most people thanked me for their new knowledge about herbs and plants. A few asked for a reminder of what to use and when. Anna and I shared a long hug that started easily, filled with love and admiration and ended with an awkward sadness. I did not give or receive many hugs in my life but this one felt special. It was difficult to look Anna in the eyes knowing I would never see her again.

"Thank you for all you have done to assist me." I gathered my strength and lifted my eyes to meet hers. "You will never know how much it means to me."

Instead of turning away and waving her hand at me, she smiled.

"Let's go, Mercy," Calum called.

I pulled on my pack and followed him. I stopped when I saw Henderson and MacIain.

"I cannot tell you how much I appreciate you both."

"Donnae let Calum get you lost," MacIain said. Normally when someone from the clan made fun of Calum or teased him, it would upset me. In my time with them, however, I had grown to learn that the Glencoe MacDonalds show affection in their own way.

"Make your family proud, lass," the seannachie said, a normal encouraging phrase for the clan but one that I had never heard directed at me.

As we turned to leave, a man came into the village. He was large, good-looking and wore the Glencoe tartan but did not look familiar. I thought I heard a few people whisper "Alasdair" but I could not be sure. He walked straight up to Calum but said nothing. Calum looked stricken and pale, as if he needed to vomit. He swallowed hard before speaking.

"Sir," Calum said.

The man hugged him. He wrapped both arms around Calum and squeezed so hard I thought Calum would be crushed. When he pulled back, they both had tears in their eyes. I wondered if Calum's were from the physical pain of being hugged that hard.

"I was up near Tain when the lads told me you were here but were not staying. I traveled day and night without food or rest. I couldnae give up the chance to thank you in person."

Calum shook his head and stared at the ground.

"I cannae thank you enough, son," the man said. "She could be alive and well and it's because of you."

Alasdair. The father of the girl Calum had taken to Greenock to board a ship in order to live with family in America. No one knew what became of her.

Calum stared at the ground a beat longer then lifted his head.

"I wish I could have done more, sir," he said.

"Alasdair." He put out his hand and Calum shook it. "You have earned the right to call me Alasdair. Go on, son. It seems there is another lass in need of your help." He turned to me. "Good luck to you. You are in good hands with Calum."

Calum began walking again and, again, the clanspeople called out good wishes for our journey. I followed Calum out of the village and into the fields that led to the sleeping dragons.

Chapter Thirty Six

We moved quickly, with Calum still pointing out potential hazards and it still annoying me. Had I not proven my worth? Had I tripped even once since that first one during our escape from the animals? It amazed me how much more irritating Calum was when we were alone.

By sunset on the first day, I had no idea how far we had traveled but the terrain had changed considerably. We were not yet in the thickest part of the woods but we were getting nearer. We were climbing a rather steep portion of a small hill when we heard something in a nearby bush. Calum stopped and listened. The noises continued. It sounded to me like it was several people making a similar climb but in the other direction. Calum motioned to me to keep low and resumed our climb.

"Will they not hear us?" I asked.

"If you keep talking they will."

I took his meaning and shut my mouth. It was quite frightening. Having no idea who the other people were, my mind came up with all kinds of possibilities. Were they thieves? British soldiers who hated Glencoe MacDonalds? Cattle-rustlers from another clan who also hated Glencoe MacDonalds? No matter who was on the other side of the bushes, we had to chance being discovered and continue to climb. There was so little time.

We had been hiking for many hours when I saw a loch. It looked familiar, although I had no idea as to why. Calum stopped at the water's edge.

"We need to rest for a short bit, get some food and water."

I sat on a nearby rock, took off my shoe to rub my club foot, and continued to look around. The surroundings reminded me of the loch where we had met MacIain.

"Is this where we first saw your chief?" I asked.

"Aye."

"We are going back from where we came?" I asked. I knew we had wasted time by not going straight to the proper location of Stirling Castle, but it had not occurred to me that we would be back-tracking on the exact ground where we had been.

"Aye. For some of the trip. We'll pass Loch Eirann, too." Calum was answering in short sentences which meant he was trying to get me to stop asking questions. There was information he did not want me to have.

"Where you found me? How far from Stirling Castle was I that day?"

Calum pretended to be absorbed with searching his pack for food.

"Calum?" I asked in a quiet voice but one that he knew meant I expected a true answer.

"A day and a half," he said. "At most. Take a big drink from your canteen and refill it. We need to move soon."

A day and a half. At most. Part of my brain wanted to show anger, throw things, scream, even cry but somehow I stayed calm. No reason to throw a fit that would do no good. I had to conserve my energy for traveling. Perhaps there would be time later to reflect on the absurdity of going so far in the wrong direction when my goal was but a day and half from the crash.

To distract myself, I examined the plants near the few small trees in the area.

"What are you looking for? You have herbs for headaches and pains, right?"

"Aye, but there are different plants here. These will help with our stomachs."

"Grab some and let's get moving. We will walk through most of the night. Are there any plants that will help us stay awake?"

"Aye, of course."

We walked in near silence for hours. I have no idea what thoughts were going through Calum's head. Cursing his own honor as well as the day he met me, probably. I was wondering why he continued to help me. He had not only discharged any basic requirement of his personal code of conduct but had gone far and away beyond it. Was there something he wanted from me? Something for which he could not ask until he had done what he thought was enough to earn it? Perhaps he was reluctant to inquire before he knew the answer to another question.

"Why do you not ask me?"

"Ask you what?"

A black butterfly whose wings were ringed in reddish-orange with white spots on the tips fluttered toward me. It landed on my arm. I tried not to move it too much as I felt the tiny legs touch my skin through my sleeve.

"If I am a witch?"

The butterfly left my arm and continued its journey. Calum and I walked in complete silence, as if I had not spoken the unspeakable word. There had been massive witch hunts in Scotland in the past. At least a thousand people had been rounded up and killed due to accusations of witchcraft. Speaking with someone suspected of such crimes was, itself, a serious offense, punishable by death under the 1563 Witchcraft Act in Scotland. Even saying the word could cause an enormous amount of trouble. Yet, Calum did not flinch, did not scold me for saying it. He did not react in any negative way. Or positive way, come to that.

"You must have wondered," I continued since he would not. "You must have noticed that my knowledge and skill with plants and insects is greater than any other healer you have met. Why do you not ask me?"

Again, we walked along in silence, although this time Calum picked up his speed. I could not determine if the quickened pace was a result of his anger at my pressing him on a dangerous conversation or if he simply wanted to be free of me as soon as possible. I was considering what I would say next when Calum spoke.

"I do not ask because I do not wish to know."

Chapter Thirty Seven

I was aware of the cold ground first, then the fact that my neck had a painful cramp in it. I opened my eyes and took assessment of my surroundings. I was alone in the woods, still had not completed my task, and still had to rely on Calum. Where was he anyway? I stood to get a better view but did not see him. The trees blocked out what little moonlight there had been so we had been forced to stop and rest. I noticed Calum's travel sack on the ground and we were near a small burn for water so I knew he could not have gone far. Perhaps he had gone to relieve himself.

When we were in the safety of the glen, he had left me alone, or with Anna, most of the time, whether I was awake or asleep. Being out in the woods again, I felt uneasy in his absence. I greatly disliked feeling that way but I could not deny it. Where had he gone? Had he finally had enough of my impossible journey and ditched me here in the middle of nowhere? What if a miscreant comes upon me? How could Calum leave me with no way to defend myself?

I was about to accept that scenario and get ready to restart the journey on my own when Calum strode back into view. From that distance, I could not make out what he carried in his hands. As he got closer, the objects came more in to focus. When he was almost upon me, I saw for certain what he held. They were my small satchel and his beloved canteen. Both had been lost in our altercation with the thief before we reached Glencoe.

"How did you get these? Is this where you were? Is this why you left me?"

"I think you know. Aye, and aye."

"What about the thief?"

"He donnae need them anymore." He dropped my satchel at my feet and walked over to the burn. He filled his newly-reclaimed canteen, drank deeply from it and filled it again. Then he let the water wash over his blood-stained hands.

The outside of the satchel looked to be in good shape except for singe marks from the accident and where the strap had broken and been tied back together. The break must have happened when I lost it. I wondered if the thief had mended it or Calum.

"Is the poem inside?" I asked.

Calum shrugged.

I opened the satchel and pulled my face away as a terrible odor escaped from the opening.

"Ack! What was he keeping in here?" I turned it upside down and a number of things fell out including what appeared to be dried leaves, a toad who was still alive, and the foot of a rabbit who was most likely not.

"Looks like he thought it was his good luck bag," Calum said. "Not for long."

I ignored his comment, although I agreed with it, and felt for the false panel in the satchel. When I touched it, it crunched a little. Paper. That was a good sign. I ripped open the panel and pulled out the paper with the poem. Relief flooded my body. It was all working out. Three more days of walking and I would be able to do what I had been sent to do. I was ready to travel with renewed spirit and cheery attitude.

"Are there any special plants here that you want before we get moving?" Calum asked. He ended his sentence with a bit of a yawn.

I did a little quick figuring in my head and realized that Calum had not slept, at least not for more than an hour. He had to be exhausted. He was also grabbing at his side and wincing as he did.

"Is that a new injury or the old one?"

"No matter, either way. Let's go."

I wanted to get moving even more than he did but he obviously needed rest.

"Calum, let me look at it." I hoped I could get him to sit for a few minutes while I checked his injury, maybe long enough to make him a good poultice for it.

"Later." He picked up his pack and started walking. I could not make him accept my help. I draped my satchel over my shoulders, picked up my pack and followed.

Chapter Thirty Eight

The natural growth in the woods when spring turned to summer gave us many more plants and animals to deal with than our first trek through. Calum did his best to warn me of potential threats but he seemed distracted. We walked for hours and hours without saying anything to each other. Calum would point out certain obstacles but said nothing. As much as I resented it when he did, there was one time when he failed to point out a vine and I stumbled over it. He shot me a look of annoyance but said nothing.

I was not used to thinking about our journey's path nor had I any knowledge of where it would lead, other than Stirling Castle's King's Knot garden. I was surprised when I looked up and saw something I recognized.

I took a sip from my canteen to moisten my dry throat before attempting to speak after so many hours of silence.

"Is that what I think it is?" I asked.

Calum stumbled a little on a rock then nodded.

A small trail of smoke rose from what seemed to be a series of trees. Calum and I knew better. It was Bear Man's house. I actually knew where I was and had an idea how to get back to the loch as Calum had said we would.

It was not long after that when I noticed a distinct change in Calum's behavior. He started muttering to himself, or at least I thought it was to himself as it was nowhere near loud enough for me to hear. He stumbled a few more times. Worry for his health and safety dominated my thoughts and, I am ashamed to admit, concern that if he were to become truly ill, we would not make it to Stirling in time to deliver my message and find out about my family.

"Maybe we could rest for a spell?" I asked, hoping that if I could get him to sit, I could make a poultice for his injury and perhaps a good tea.

"No," he said. "We have to cover more ground before dark. It gets too dark."

That last sentence did not sound like Calum.

"I think we should stop. You are acting strange."

"There is nothing wrong with me! I am well, thank you."

"You are not well. You are sweating and moving at a slow pace."

"If I am not moving fast enough for your liking, you are free to… you are free to…you know, go on…"

"Calum?"

He fell, not completely to the ground, but his legs failed him and he landed on his knees. I tried to catch him as he went down, but was only able to grab hold of one of his arms. I pulled on that sweaty arm, trying to get him back to his feet and that was when I saw it. The wound he had suffered from our altercation with the thief in the woods was oozing green puss. It was infected.

This was bad. Really, really bad. Fever caused by the infection had overtaken Calum's body. Nothing I had gathered would be strong enough. There was only one plant I had seen on our journey that had any hope with a fever this strong. I needed to make a tea from the bark of the white willow tree. I had to get to Loch Eirann as fast as possible.

Calum was in no condition to walk another step, much less all the way to the loch. I had no choice but to call on an old friend. I prayed he would be home.

"Over here, Calum," I said as I half-lead, half-carried him to a large clump of bushes. "Rest here until I get back."

"No, Dory," he said in a soft voice, "I won't leave you this time. We have to stay together."

Perfect. Now he was delusional. I tugged him to the ground, laid out his blanket as close to the bushes as I could and rolled him on to it. I hoped no thieves or other ne'er-do-wells happened upon him in my absence.

"I will return as soon as possible. Do try not to call attention to yourself."

He mumbled something at me as I took off back in the direction of Bear Man and his broken down horse. It was the fastest I had ever run. It had to be. Calum's life depended on it.

Chapter Thirty Nine

P lease be home. Please be home. Please be home. I did not want to think about what would happen if Bear Man was not in his lop-sided abode. My first stop was the small barn. Garry turned his head and snorted at me when I peeked into his stall. Good. Now to get Bear Man on board. I stood in front of his door, straightened my skirts, and took a deep breath. I needed to seem calm and relaxed, not urgent. Bear Man did not respond well to quick thinking. After one more deep breath, I knocked.

There was no response. I knocked again. No response again. I pressed my ear to the thick wooden door. Did I hear something inside the small house? Or did I just want to hear it? I knocked again, this time louder and less polite.

"Hello!!!" I called through the door. "Are you home? Sir?"

Again, I pressed my ear to the door. Shuffling sounds. From inside, I could hear definite shuffling noises. Bear Man was home!

"Hello. Hello, sir. It is Mercy. Calum's friend. We were here a few weeks ago. I require your assistance, if you are able. Calum, really."

The shuffling sounds got louder as Bear Man neared the door.

"Greetings, lass," Bear Man said at my approach. "I thought I had seen the last of you."

"I hope it is alright that we returned, sir," I said.

"Yes, yes," he said after he heaved open the creaking door. "Did you say the lad needs help?"

I nodded. "We are traveling again and Calum has fallen ill. I fear he has a strong fever brought on by an infected wound suffered while defending me from a thief."

"Oh, my. Fevers are quite dangerous. But I'm no healer like you."

"Aye, sir. I know what plants I need to help him but I need assistance getting to them with enough haste." I paused, unsure of how to phrase my request. "How is your horse, sir?"

"Garry? You need Garry? Yes, yes, of course. Please, if Garry can help you and your young lad then by all means take him! Although I'm afraid he is a bit too broken down to be too fast."

"I am sure he will make our journey easier. Oh, thank you so much! Calum will return Garry as soon as he can."

"That old horse is more of a companion than a work animal at this point. If he can be of service elsewhere, please let him be."

I wanted to grab the reins and start my journey back to Calum but something was nagging at my brain. Calum would not allow this inequitable trade. Inside, I groaned. I had to give Bear Man something in order to take Garry, whether he thought I did or not.

"Sir, I cannot take him without a trade. I have little time. Is there a task I can do for you before I return to Calum?"

"Well, let's see," Bear Man said at a slow pace. I tried to remain calm as inside my mind I was screaming at him to hurry.

"That poultice helped my back a great deal," he said. "Can you make me another?"

"Of course! I need supplies."

I took off around the outside of the house to the water. I gathered comfrey, feverfew, and a little Queen of the Meadow, in case he had stomach troubles. On the way back around to the door I saw an orange, black and yellow butterfly cross my path. I followed it to a bit of heather growing out from the base of the house. A poultice of this would do his rheumatism aches well so I grabbed a bit.

"Do I have to do anything to it?" Bear Man asked when I returned with the plants.

"Steep it in hot water for a few minutes, soak a rag with it and place it on your back. Is that all you want in return for Garry?"

"You've helped me greatly with your knowledge of plants. Please, take Garry and get back to your lad. I have no idea how that broken-down beast will be able to help you. Maybe you can make him some plant tea or something."

"Thank you, sir!" I called to him as I crossed the small space to the door in one long stride. "I thank you!"

"Aye, yeah." I heard him say as I closed the door behind me then ran for the barn.

"Okay, Garry," I said as I slowed my pace and got closer to the horse. "We have to help Calum." I placed my hand on his neck and rubbed his hair. It was matted in some places and there were spots missing where insects had eaten away at him. It was clear the Bear Man had not taken good care of this beautiful animal.

Garry snorted a little when my hand grazed one of the bare spots on his neck.

"Sorry," I said. "I meant no harm. I'll make you an ointment to help that feel better. In fact it should help you feel better in many places."

I unhooked his reins and led Garry out of his enclosure and into the woods outside his home. We walked at a slow pace as he was unable to go any faster. I took him to the water where the Bear Man had given me his canteen all those days ago on our first visit to this place. Garry bent his long neck down toward the water and drank from the burn. There was little chance that Garry could get far from me so I released his reins.

I looked through the herbs in my bag and chose the best pickings of the plants I needed. This had to be the best ointment I had ever made. All the while, my mind was on Calum and whether he would still be under that bush when I returned. I crushed herbs with my fingers against the palm of my hand and little by little added enough water to make it smooth but not too much. Once I had the consistency I wanted, I walked a few short steps to Garry. He turned his massive head in my direction as I approached him.

"Okay, Garry," I said. "You must trust I am only doing this for

Calum. This is going to feel a little weird. Do not fret, my dear friend. It will not hurt you but it will make you feel strange for a while. I do not like to do this to you, but Calum's infection is quite bad. We need to save his life."

As I spoke soft, kind words to him, I rubbed the ointment first on his neck and then through his mangy mane of hair. Garry did not snort, he did not pull away. In fact he did not react much at all. By the time I had used the final bit of ointment to mold his forelock into a point that stuck straight up between his eyes, Garry started to move a bit. His breathing seemed to get stronger and his eyes seemed to focus on me.

"I know, Garry," I said out loud, "but we have to help Calum."

I dipped my canteen in the water to fill it then got on Garry's back and pointed him in the direction of Calum. We did not have much time. Calum needed us.

With every step, Garry got stronger and moved with more confidence. He made his way through the forest with ease and grace. I laid my head on the side of his neck and pressed my body as close to his as possible. I held on and let Garry move on his own with a few directional corrections. It felt freeing to be on Garry's back as he took us through the woods and back to Calum.

When we approached the clump of bushes where I had left Calum, I pulled on Garry's reins to get him to slow his pace. Before we reached the edge of the clearing, I stopped him and dismounted. I wrapped the reins around a tree but had no true fear of Garry taking off without me. I walked gingerly to where I had left Calum. To my relief, he was still there. He was much paler and sweatier but still there.

"Calum?" I said in a quiet voice. "Calum, you have to wake up. Come on Calum, get up."

I repeated myself several times, increasing the loudness of my voice each time. Calum stirred but took a long time to focus on what I was saying.

"You have to stand up so we can get on Garry."

"Who?"

"Garry. Bear Man's horse."

"That old horse cannae carry us."

"Open your eyes! Look at him."

Calum rolled to his side and forced his eyes to open a teeny bit. Then they opened wide, much wider.

"What did you do?" he asked.

I shrugged, then I reached down to tug on his arm, trying to encourage him to his feet.

"Mercy." His speech was slurred but he got to his knees. "You turned him into a unicorn?" His voice went into a high squeak sound at the end of the last word. He turned to look at me. "We will be seen."

"Not if we hurry," I said, still trying to get him to stand. He was too heavy for me to move on my own. "Come on, we have to get you on the horse."

"Oh, sure," he said in a mocking tone I had not heard him use before, "I'll hop on the back of a unicorn and strut into Stirling Palace demanding to speak to a silver man about the King's Knot. No problem. Sounds like fun. Let's do it."

I knew the sarcasm was the fever talking. It had weakened both his physical and mental well-being so I decided to pretend he was being serious.

"Stupendous idea, Calum!" I said, guiding him off the ground and to the horse, pushing his bottom over the hump of Garry's back. I climbed up in front of him.

"Garry, go!"

Chapter Forty

Calum gave me a good idea how to get back to the loch. Then, he collapsed on my back with the shoulder portion of his kilt over his head. I leaned forward on to Garry's neck which now featured thickened muscles. It was a reversal of how we arrived in Glencoe.

Squirrels ran up the tree trunks and along branches while voles and mice and who-knows-what scurried through the wet, drippy, thick-smelling forest making travel more difficult. Garry had to slow from time to time to avoid overgrowth on the ground, creeks or burns, and low-hanging vines. Even with the obstacles, he moved us through the woods much faster than we could have gone ourselves, thanks to the lotion I made for him.

Ahead, there was a large stand of overgrown trees with bright light behind it. I knew that meant the loch was on the other side of those trees. I pulled on Garry's reins to slow his pace. Letting a delusional Calum see Garry in this shape was one thing, but I could not allow anyone else to see him this way. Careful not to disturb the groaning Calum any more than I had to, I managed to dismount from Garry and tie his reins as tight as I could to the sturdiest looking tree limb. Then I took off for the water's edge, dodging tree branches and hopping over tree roots, moving as fast as I could without falling.

I broke through the tree line and stopped to take in my surroundings. Beautiful plants framed a shimmering loch. Luckily no one else was there to witness the idyllic scene. I scanned the bank to the left and saw a majestic white willow tree with its blooming branches bending toward the water, the lowest ones dipped in the loch. I collected all that I needed from the tree and its bark. I took three times the amount I thought I would use. These trees were not common and I had to guess at how often Calum would require a dosage. I filled my canteen and then Calum's which I had taken from him when I dismounted Garry.

Ducking under the tree branches, back into the forest, I was relieved to see both Garry and Calum, although Calum had managed to get himself off Garry. He was standing next to the horse, staring at him.

"Sit down, Calum."

To my surprise, he obeyed without a word, even leaned against a rock. I gathered all the items I would need for a small fire, including Calum's flint which I had taken while removing his thin canteen. The fire started without much delay and I poured water from my canteen into a pot from the MacGregor travel pack. As the water heated, I placed some of the bark on a large rock and grabbed a second, somewhat smaller one. With the second rock, I pounded the bark until it broke into smaller pieces. Once the water boiled, I swept the pieces into my hand and tossed them in the water to make a tea.

"Why is Garry a unicorn?" Calum asked. "Unicorns are not real. Garry is. How can a real thing be a not real thing?"

"Do not worry, Calum. Everything is fine."

While the tea steeped, I took the water that was left from my canteen and rinsed Garry's mane. Garry whinnied and shook his neck in protest.

"Sorry, Garry, I know," I told him. "Calum has his tea but we still have time to get to Stirling. I cannot risk anyone seeing your head like this."

Garry whinnied again but did not shake his neck. I left the ointment on the rest of his body. We would still need his strong legs to get to Stirling.

When Garry's mane was wet and lying flat on his neck, I rummaged through my pack and found two apples and two rags. I fed one apple to Garry and took the other to Calum. The tea was ready. I pulled the pot off the fire and set in on a rock to cool a bit.

"What will you eat?" he asked.

"We have another apple," I replied. "I will eat after I am finished."

After pouring a good amount of tea into a tin cup, I tossed in a few bits of spearmint because white willow bark was quite bitter and I needed Calum to drink all of it. To the tea left in the pot, I added comfrey.

"Drink up," I ordered as I handed the cup to Calum. "You may drink it slowly but you must drink it all."

I watched Calum take the first sip. He made an awful bitter face but took another sip without prompting. Satisfied he would obey my orders, it was time for the next part. I dunked one of the rags from the pack in the still steaming liquid in the pot.

"Did you finish the tea?" I asked.

Calum turned the cup upside down to prove it was now empty.

"Good. Now lift up your shirt."

"What?"

"Lift up your shirt so I can see your wound."

Calum looked like his mind was still not fully engaged. That would also account for him following my directions with little resistance. He pulled his shirt out from where it was tucked into his kilt but seemed to forget why he was doing so and sat there with his hands in his lap. No matter, I could do the rest myself.

Bringing the hot pot closer to Calum, I lifted his shirt high enough to expose the entire wound. It was much worse than I thought. So bad, in fact, I worried if my poultice would be enough to pull the infection out of his body.

"Um," I said. "This will hurt."

I grabbed the poultice and slapped it on his wound as fast as I could so he could not pull away. I grabbed the other rag and used it to push the first rag hard onto his body.

"AAAAAHHHHH! AAAAAHHHHH!"

Calum's screams carried throughout the woods and out to the shores of the loch but I did not ease the pressure. If I had any chance of getting the infection out of Calum's body, I had to keep the poultice as firm against the wound as possible. With the other hand, I poured the cooler water from Calum's canteen into the pot to lower the temperature of the liquid. I removed the second rag, the one not touching the wound and put it in the diluted mix, keeping my hand on the first rag, pressing firm.

"Now, this is going to feel weird." I told him.

I peeled the first rag off his body, as slow as possible. I looked at the wound for a second before slapping on the other rag, now drenched in diluted, cooler tea. Calum winced and rolled his eyes but said nothing.

"I need you to hold this in place."

Calum did not respond.

"Calum," I repeated louder. "Put your hand here."

This time, he complied. I went back to my pack and found my light shawl. I could not remember ever being without it. I grabbed it at both sides of the main seam and pulled, ripping it apart. I continued to pull and rip until I had several long strips of fabric. I tied the ends together to create one long length.

"Okay," I told Calum. "Keep your hand in place until I tell you to move it. Understand?"

He nodded.

I placed one end of the length near Calum's hand and wrapped the rest around his body, tucking and weaving the wrapping through itself to be sure it stayed in place. When I ran out of length, I tucked the end in the other layers.

"You can drop your hand."

"What did you do?"

"I gave you white willow tea then added comfrey for a poultice to pull out the infection. It looked better after the first compress."

He looked at the ground where I had discarded the first rag. It was disgusting, bloody with green and white slime running through it. Calum vomited without warning, adding grossness to the already gross.

"Easy," I said. "You have to relax."

"Tha-that rag pulled all of that out of my body?"

"That rag and the herbs and plants infused in it."

"You got more, right? In case I need another one later?"

"Of course I did." I tucked a small bough of white willow in Calum's pack. Even the smell of it would help in his recovery. "For now, get a bit of rest."

"I won't need it," he said. "I'll be stronger soon."

"Fine," I replied. "Rest."

"Right," Calum said, leaning back into the rock and closing his eyes.

"Fine."

Chapter Forty One

I knew my destination was close and lay to the south and east of our present location, but I did not know the specific route. Neither, of course, did Garry. I needed Calum to be awake and thinking clear to get me where I needed to be.

Calum needed rest. If I moved Calum too quickly, his infection could spread and he could become even sicker. He could even die. If I did not get to Stirling in time, many people would suffer from the collapse of the Alliance and I would never find out about my family. I would be lost and alone forever.

Calum needed to sleep and I needed to move. With Garry's assistance we had traveled faster than expected for the first part of the trip. By my calculations we had about two days left to get to Stirling by the deadline. I had been forced to accept Calum's assistance throughout the journey and now he had no choice but to trust that I could help him. We had become partners in this mission and we had to rely on each other.

After cleaning up the aftermath of Calum's treatment, I rearranged our little camp so Calum was lying in a more comfortable position, covered with our meager possessions, near the fire. I sat across from him, watching to be sure he was still breathing. Garry settled himself, seeming to understand that we were not going anywhere anytime soon.

Every sound the forest made caused me to jump in fear. I passed the hours by changing a damp cloth on Calum's hot forehead, moving the white willow bough closer and closer to his nose, practicing the poem, and praying his health would improve. His life hung in immediate danger because of me. If he died, it was entirely my fault.

My mind also thought about all the people, whom I had been taught were savages, who had offered anything they could to a stranger, a lost girl from London. My whole life, I had two goals, both wrapped up in my ability to complete this mission: continue the Alliance and find out about my family. My motivation for slogging through all those lessons and weaving until my fingers were raw was not some ancient society which may or may not still exist. I thought they would know about my family, that they might be able to tell me about them so I would know why I was the way I was. I wanted to belong somewhere.

My mind was split. Part of me itched to get moving toward Stirling and part of me worried about Calum's infection. I was trapped, beholden to a legacy by people I did not know and responsible for the life of someone who had not known me when he put his life in jeopardy for me. Calum and his clans were the closest I had ever had to family. I would not betray their trust. I would not betray Calum.

I chided myself for still hoping we would make it to Stirling. Calum was what mattered now. In my secret heart, I wished for Calum to get better, for us to make it to Stirling on time, recite the poem, deliver the woven message, and to learn about my parents and their families. I wished that if all that happened, it would be worth it. I hoped that this entire terrible journey would result in something good.

I tried to doze off and on, stirring to tend to Calum, feed Garry, or just to move. After weeks of constant movement and hard work, sitting around for hours and hours was taxing on my body. I never strayed far for fear that I would miss hearing Calum's call for assistance. During one of my dozing times, Garry's whinnying woke me. It was still dark. Calum was stirring which is likely what caused Garry to whinny.

"What day is it?"

Without responding, I poked the fire and made him another cup of white willow tea. He took it and drank without questioning.

"Has your fever returned?" I asked.

"No," he said. "You watched me drink more of that nasty tea."

I looked at him, assessing whether he was well enough to tell the difference between being sick or well.

"Do not come over here," he warned.

"What?" I asked, knowing full well what he meant.

"Do not come over here and feel my head."

"I have no intention of touching your sweaty forehead," I lied but enjoyed the fact that he was well enough to spar with me. "But why are you afraid I would?"

"I'm not afraid. I just don't want your dirty smelly hands on me."

"Fine. Then lift your shirt."

"What?"

"Are we really going to do this again? Come on."

He rolled his eyes and sighed. He did, however, put his canteen on the ground and lift his shirt, peeking over the edge of the cloth to get a good look at it himself.

"Not too bad," I said, careful not to touch it. The area all around the wound and the wound itself would be quite tender and I did not want to hurt Calum even though he had called my hands dirty and smelly. "It will feel better after the next poultice."

"Next poultice?" Calum asked in an alarmed voice. "No way. I was out of my mind last time you did that. There is no way I'm letting you do it again!"

"Of course not. You will do it this time. You are much stronger and can get the deep infection out by pressing even harder than I ever could."

"I'm not going to press a poultice into my wound!"

"Fine. I will do it, then."

We were silent for a while as Calum realized how I had tricked him.

"Right. We'll see."

He sat back a bit and closed his eyes. I concentrated on his breathing, trying to determine if it was even. Suddenly his eyelids flew open.

"You didn't tell me what day it is," he said. "How long was I out?"

"Calm yourself, Calum," I said. "You still need rest. By my count, it is either very late on the twentieth or quite early on the twenty first."

My response took a few seconds to sink in for Calum.

"We have less than a day to get there?" Calum asked, his voice shaky but loud.

"Aye, yeah." My response was calm and quiet.

Calum jumped to his feet. A good sign for his recovery but he swooned a bit once he was upright.

"We have to get moving!" he yelled. "We may not have enough time to get there!"

"We cannot move until you are strong enough," I told him. My voice held a calm I did not feel inside.

He locked his eyes on mine and I did not blink. I had put my life's work in jeopardy in order to guard his life. He was willing to risk his life for me to complete my life's mission.

"I can rest as we ride, assuming you haven't broken Garry."

It was difficult not to grin at his verbal jab about Garry because it made me so happy to hear him be ornery again. Instead, I nodded.

"Let's go."

Chapter Forty Two

W e rode like before, me in front holding Garry's reins, Calum in the back. Although this time he rested less and gave more instructions. Too many instructions, pointing out possible barriers and dips in the path as he had while we were walking. Once in a while, I rolled my eyes as he could not see me.

We moved at a rapid pace. Garry enjoyed his strength and showed off how fast he could move. We did not stop for meals, instead Calum passed forward my share of what was left in the travel pack. I thought about stopping to feed Garry but we did not have any more apples. I hoped the lotion would give him the strength to get us there on time.

"You have to be there by midnight?" he asked.

"Aye."

"Is it by midnight or at midnight?" he asked.

That was an excellent question that I had not considered. My hands started to sweat. Mr. Willicks had us on track to be here many, many days in advance but that did not mean I could have given the message when we arrived. He might have aimed to arrive early to be sure we were not late. When traveling long distances it was difficult to predict how long a journey would take. Was midnight at midsummer the exact date and time of the meeting or a deadline?

"I have no idea," I confessed.

"How will we get in the castle?" I asked. Why had I not thought of these questions before now?

"The King's garden that holds the King's Knot is on the castle grounds, not within the fortress of the castle. It lies to the south in one of the lower fields. It is not vital during a siege so there was no need or room, probably, to build within the castle walls."

"How much further?" I asked as the darkness deepened.

"A few miles."

I controlled Garry's reins and Calum gave directions. With his lotion still energizing his muscles, Garry moved like a much younger horse. My mind, however, was spinning even faster. We had made it this far. What if this was the wrong thing to be doing? What if I needed to finish delivering the message, the whole message, by midnight? What if I messed up at the last moment? What if I failed?

To distract myself, I tried to recall the poem, now nestled in the returned satchel pressed against my hip.

The woods gave way to open fields with tufts of grey-brown grasses and squishier ground. I had come to learn that an unexpected marsh now and then was not unusual in Scotland. We trotted past a couple of older women carrying water jugs and a basket of clothing. Calum pulled his cloak around him when he saw them. I was not certain why.

"We will be coming to town soon," he said.

I nodded. Soon. Soon, I would be put to the most intense test of my life, the one test for which I had been training since my first memories. Soon, I would learn of my family. Worry filled my body. Would I come this far and still miss my chance? Calum pointed to our right and I could see the castle. Perched atop an impressive crag, the castle was the very picture of wealth and dominance. It was intimidating and inspiring all at once.

I would make it there by midnight, for sure. Was that soon enough? The marshlands became more solid ground. We passed through fields of large coos with their shaggy red, orange, brown hair and large horns, then fluffy sheep, their coats having grown back after the spring shearing. Many turned their little heads in our direction as Garry bounded through their home but only one or two bleated at us.

"How much longer until we reach the gardens?" I asked as loud as I could without shouting.

"It's just after the animal fields."

We were even closer than I had thought. I felt faint from nervousness. I looked up again at the castle and noticed smoke, loads of it, coming from one location.

"Calum!" I shouted in spite of myself.

"The bonfires have started!" Calum called. "Midsummer is almost here! We must hurry to the knot."

We left the sheep behind and entered a new section, which was an ornamental garden with no flowers. Before us was an enormous open field. From the height of Garry's back I could see squared-off rings of small, flat expanses, creating a step-like structure. I pulled Garry's reins to signal him to stop while Calum and I dismounted almost simultaneously. We joined hands and ran together into the area known as the King's Knot.

The view was different without Garry's height. From the ground it looked like a line of evenly-spaced steps creating a large mound. A well-worn path led us up the layers to the center. We did not break stride as we climbed each steep section until we reached the top.

Calum and I stopped, frozen in confusion on the top layer. Standing in the rounded center of the knot stood a single figure dressed in a long robe with a hood covering the head and most of the face. Had the figure been there moments earlier? He (or she) held a lit torch and motioned for us to come closer. My heart would not calm down. Calum and I took slow steps, still hand-in-hand, until the figure's arm raised to tell us to stop. Darkness and the flickering torch obscured my sight but I thought I saw the handle of a sword tucked into the figure's belt.

My heart raced so loud inside my body I was certain both of them could hear it. Calum did not reach for his weapon although he continued to grip his free hand into a fist and then extend his fingers, then grip it again.

The figure nodded, which I guessed was my signal to recite the poem. I squeezed Calum's hand then dropped it. My nerves made my voice shake.

"With righteous mane and handsome horn,

Once born of myth to clean the slate,

The swift, courageous unicorn

Will be the one to seal our fate."

Garry snorted from the lower field after I finished. I wished he would be still.

The figure nodded again, turned, then headed down the other side of the knot. Calum glanced at me and shrugged. We followed the figure who moved with surprising speed. I took a better look at the castle. It sat upon an enormous rocky cliff and the castle's stone walls stretched upward from there. Were we expected to climb that cliff? There was no way I could do that, neither could Calum in his current state. Plus, Garry would have to stay at the bottom.

Garry caught up with us as we traversed an open field and were soon in a forest at the base of the cliff. The figure walked straight toward the largest, oldest-looking tree in the woods. I worried the figure was lost because it did not attempt to veer from the tree, instead walking straight for the center. I looked at Calum who looked as confused as I felt. Perhaps we were to rest on the tree before our ascent up the enormous cliff face?

The figure stopped at the base of the tree, raised a hand and pushed on the bark. It moved. Not the whole tree, but part of the bark moved open like a door.

"The horse cannot go further," said the figure, whose voice sounded female. "He will be brought another way."

I pulled his reins in tight to nuzzle his nose. Leaving Garry felt like a cruel thing to do. How did I know what would happen to him? Could I trust this strange figure? Who would be taking him? I did not see any one else in the forest. I looked at Calum.

"He will be okay," he whispered but his eyes did not seem convinced. I could not jeopardize the mission because of Garry, even though he had been crucial in getting us this far. I stepped to the side and wrapped his reins around one of the low branches of the large tree. I kissed him on his nose. He snorted.

The figure reached inside the cavity of the tree and placed the torch in a holder on what appeared to be a wall, then disappeared down some stairs. Calum motioned for me to go first.

Chapter Forty Three

The tree turned out to be the opening of a spiral, stone passage. We descended for a couple of turns before the steps leveled out and then went straight up with a landing every thirty steps or so that changed the direction of the stairs by a quarter turn. At even intervals, lit torches waited for us to pass. We walked in silence with no idea how far we had left to climb. My chest was tight from the exertion and my body slick with sweat. I feared what the climb must be doing to Calum. He had not fully recovered and the exertion could cause a setback in his recovery. Or worse.

When the staircase became spiral again, I knew we were close to the end. We were still underground. I could tell because the staircase tower did not have arrow slits or windows. The figure stopped so suddenly Calum had to put his hand on my shoulder to stop himself from colliding with me. There was an enormous door with a round iron hoop about a foot in diameter in the center. The figure raised and lowered the iron hoop, knocking on the door.

The door opened. I expected an eerie *cree-ea-kk* noise but the door slid open without a sound. We entered a room with a window that appeared to open to a hallway and then a courtyard, not the outside. In front of us stood another figure, his hood lowered so we could see his face. He nodded at me first and then Calum.

"Welcome," he said. "Are you ready for your challenge?"

Calum stepped forward, his honor forcing him to be ready to take on any challenge, but I was able to speak first.

"I will, sir," I said, "but first, I must make a request."

"That is most unusual," the man replied.

"I understand but it is necessary. This lad was injured during his efforts to escort me here. I am unharmed but he requires a soft place to rest and dragon's blood."

"Dragon's blood? There is no dragon's blood in the whole of Britain."

"Wait," Calum said. "What's dragon's blood?"

"Aye," I replied to the figure and ignored Calum, "but the castle must have some way of getting it. In fact, you must have many uses for it and keep much of it on hand."

The man did not seem angry but more impressed with my request.

"Send to the apothecary for some dragon's blood. Prepare it for use on a flesh wound."

Calum tried to protest but the people in the room fussed and brought forth a cushioned chair and a stool for his feet.

"Sit down, Calum. You need to rest." I said without moving from my spot. Someone arrived carrying a tray with a ceramic container of red tinted cream and a clean rag. "They will swipe the cream on the wound and cover it with the rag."

"What is dragon's blood?" Calum asked, confusion muddling his voice.

"The sap of a very special tree. It will heal you faster. If you stay still and rest."

Calum paused as if he wanted to speak, then nodded. I turned to the man in front of me. "I am prepared for the challenge."

"Fine, then. Your warp is waiting."

"Mercy," Calum whispered. "What are you doing? And what in the world is a warp?"

"I am fulfilling my mission. Be still and rest."

I sat down on the crude three-footed stool positioned before a table which held a simple foot-by-foot loom with thin linen strung in straight, even, vertical lines. Handsome tapestry tools – bobbins, comb-shaped beaters, and yarn shuttles – poked out of a jar beside the loom. I pulled the satchel strap from around my shoulders and dropped the bag on the ground. I folded back the top layer of my skirts at the waist and undid my bodice a tiny bit so I could reach the small pocket next to my shift. I pulled out small lengths of silken and golden yarns wrapped into butterflies for ease of weaving. They fluttered as I dropped them into my satchel, I glanced over at Calum. He looked on with caution.

Someone dressed in Highland garb brought a tray and left it on another small table I could reach from my stool. I would need the cheese, bread, fruit, mead, and bits of meat it held to sustain me while I worked. I hoped Calum would be given food as well. I wondered if anyone had gotten Garry.

Along with candles to light the space, all around the loom were dozens and dozens of large spools of wool yarn which would make up the majority of the weave I was about to create. My delicate butterfly yarns would provide finer details. The small tapestry was not an original pattern and one that I had woven many, many times during my training in London. After selecting the colors I needed, I loaded my bobbins and set to work.

While concentrating on the task at hand, it was important not to let my emotions impact me. I could not worry about what Calum was thinking, or about our arduous journey to get me here, or all the hours of my childhood spent learning to weave this exact tapestry, or about where Garry was and if anyone had fed him. I tucked and wove and passed the yarn in and out, in and out, between the warp lines. I bounced my yarn beater on sections to push the yarn together, making the white linen warp disappear. I changed colors, leaving the previous bobbins, and in some cases butterflies, hanging where they were until they were needed again. At the busiest part I had near fifteen colors attached at once. It was a complicated pattern.

Hours passed before the tapestry began to resemble anything recognizable. It was a beautiful pattern. I told myself the story as I wove in order to keep my mind focused. I could not allow myself to be distracted. The sounds of the room dropped back and I heard my own voice telling the story of the Hunt of the Unicorn.

The Hunt was a series of tapestry panels woven in Europe over a hundred years ago. The tapestries depicted a group of men hunting and capturing a unicorn. The story was symbolic, of course, as it was impossible to catch a unicorn. The original tapestries were of the highest quality but more important, they held a great secret. My tapestry sample was a reproduction of some of the plants surrounding the unicorn in one of the panels. My knowledge of plants and their healing powers was rooted in learning how to make the tapestry look as authentic as possible. I had spent as many hours studying plants as I had the weaving. My entire childhood had been geared for this moment.

Sunlight entered the window through the courtyard by the time I completed my work. I returned the tools to their spots and stood. My foot and my back ached, my arms felt like jelly and my fingers throbbed. I longed to stretch but stood stock straight with my hands in front of me, as I had been taught to do while a tapestry was judged. The man, the one who greeted us at the door, came forward and studied the tapestry. Everyone remained still and silent.

I took the moment to find Calum who was standing by a table. It looked as if he had been given food, drink and compresses while I worked. It surprised me how happy I was that he was still there and that Garry had been brought up. Our adventure together had come down to this moment, the opinion of this one man. I had no idea what would happen if he denied me. Of course, I had no true idea what would happen if he accepted me. My mission would be completed, my destiny fulfilled but what next? Back to London, to that lonely, dreary flat?

Would I get answers about my family?

Chapter Forty Four

"Extraordinary," the man said. It felt as if everyone in the room relaxed at once. I let my head hang in relief for the briefest of moments. "One of the finest renderings I have ever seen." He turned to face me. "I deem thee a proven member of the Unicorn Order."

Two men had been standing beside a large sheet draped over something. They removed the sheet with a flourish at the man's pronouncement. Underneath was the original tapestry panel from which my small section had come.

Calum looked at me and then turned to look at the large tapestry.

"It's the —" I started to explain.

"Hunt of the Unicorn."

"Truly remarkable!" the man interjected. "I must know if it is true. Tell me. What is your name?" He leaned forward, awaiting my response. I did not disappoint.

"Je suis de la maison de Laroche. My parents named me Mercredi, Mercy for short."

He banged his hands together in one loud clap while others in the room gasped, and brought their hands to their mouths, chests or heads.

"A Laroche!" one of them said.

"Not any Laroche. Her mother's family could have worked on this exact piece!"

More gasps and a little applause rose up from the gathered group. Garry snorted and flicked his right ear.

"Sir?" I asked then swallowed hard before asking my next question. "What do you know of my family?"

"Why, your parents each come from wildly talented artisan

families, famous the world over for tapestry weaving. It was even ru-
mored at one point that the king himself requested your great-grand-
mother to weave a tapestry in order to woo his intended bride!"

Everyone smiled and nodded. It was clearly a well-known tale.

"But look who I am telling, right? You will be much better at
telling your own noble family's history. Please, do tell us all that you
know! You must have such glorious tales to tell! Do you have a deformed foot, as well?"

My deformity was a family trait? It was a connection to the family
I would never know? Blasted tears sprung to my eyes. I tried to keep
them from falling.

"Sir," I answered. "I have no tales. My parents were killed when I
was an infant. I never knew them." The jovial atmosphere in the room
shrunk, pity grew in its place. "I was sent to London to live with my
uncle. He knew about my life's mission and hired the best tutors to
train me but he never, ever spoke of my parents."

"Oh, child," said the woman who had met us at the King's Knot.
She had lowered her hood and stood near the male figure.

"That explains your accent," the man said. "You were able to weave
like that without direct instructions from your parents. What an incredible talent!"

"And, what a sad story," the woman added. "When we are finished
with this business you will sit and eat a proper meal while we delight
you with the glories of your family! We have much to teach you of
your ancestors."

My heart lightened. I would finally hear of the generations that
came before me. The feeling inside was not the elation I expected.
I was excited to hear the stories and proud that I had completed my
mission but it felt…empty. This was all in the past. How would it
influence my future?

"You spoke of more business?" Calum asked, stepping forward
from his chair.

"Oh, yes, of course," the lead man said. "Pardon my exuberance. My name is Conrad Milshireson and it was a true pleasure to watch you work." I did not know how to react so I remained silent and nodded. "The true tale of the tapestries is passed down through the members of the 'Unicorn Order.' Mercredi is a part of that heritage now and the Alliance continues."

"It would not have come to be if not for Calum," I said. Turning to him I continued. "Thank you for all that you did to get me here. Without you, I would have died at the crash site, and the Alliance would have faltered."

Everyone around us nodded. Calum crossed the room and stood beside me.

"I believe we asked what happens now?" he said. After learning of my family's history and seeing how these people treated us, he still felt the need to protect me.

"Aye. Yes. My apologies," Milshireson said as he handed me a parcel. "This was sent ahead of your arrival, from your uncle I suppose. You were to open it if you succeeded." He scoffed and looked at the others in the room. "As if there were ever any doubt. Such skill!"

Calum let out a little sound but said nothing. I set the package on the stool I had used and pulled the letter off the top. It was still closed with wax encrusted by my uncle's seal. I cracked it and read the note to Calum, knowing everyone else would hear it, too.

"I knew I could trust you to complete your mission. The Scottish-French connection, the Auld Alliance, must be kept strong and true, even in secret. Your journey from this point on is your own. Should you choose to return to London, I will welcome you home. Should Mr. Willicks return without you, I wish you well and hope you will find the time to put pen to paper and tell me of your life.

"Your parents would be quite proud of whom you have become, no thanks to me. I did my best to provide good tutors and role models other than myself, because who would want to be like me, but it was no substitute for the family

you should have had. My inability to provide that for you is my deepest regret. Instead, now, I give you all that I can, your freedom.

"Whatever your choice, you will be provided safe passage anywhere in the world plus cash and provisions to start a life when you arrive. A chaperone will be assigned to accompany you since Mr. Willicks has expressed his desire to return home as soon as possible.

"The choice is yours."

Chapter Forty Five

"Where do you want to go?" Milshireson asked. "Home to London? To your native France? Spain, Italy, America, Iceland, China? Stay here in Scotland? Anywhere at all. It is up to you."

For the first time I was being given a choice. A real choice with true consequences. A choice that would determine the course of the rest of my life. Many times I had wished for this ability. My parents had died when I was so young, I had been someone's charge, their responsibility, my whole life. Someone else was always determining my path through what was for 'the betterment of the child' and secretly what was best for the Alliance. Here, this grown man was asking me to determine for myself what I wanted to do.

I had absolutely no idea.

None.

Not a clue.

I stood for a while trying to make it look like I was weighing my options. I had no idea how I would survive alone in any country, including the one in which I currently stood.

"You can have someone return the horse to his owner, I trust?" I asked, trying to sound official while stalling for time to think.

Mr. Conrad Milshireson nodded.

I turned to Calum. "Are you going back to MacGregor?"

He shook his head. "My time with them was well spent but I will not return."

"Glencoe, then? You have earned the respect and gratitude of many of your clanspeople. Including Alasdair. Will you return to them?"

"Gratitude but respect will take a while," he corrected.

I could not believe I was asking him even as the words left my mouth.

"Would you want to go with me? They expect me to travel with a companion."

Calum looked surprised at first and then a strange smile spread across his face.

"Well," he said with slow purpose. "I happen to know someone in America." He paused for a moment. "At least, I think I do."

I smiled at his meaning. It weighed on Calum that he did not know if his friend had finished her journey across the ocean. It would bring him peace to know what happened to her as I was gaining peace by learning about my family history. America would be an interesting place to start a new life.

"All right, then," I said. "I have decided. Calum and I will go to America."

Fact versus Fiction

Historical Fiction is fiction sparked by a real person, place or event. It draws from all theories, and then uses fictional characters, places, and events to tell a new story.

The Glencoe Massacre occurred in 1692. There are many different accounts which makes getting to the absolute truth unlikely. It is generally accepted that the attack at Glencoe started just before dawn on the 13th of February 1692, was ordered by King William and carried out by Redcoats under Robert Campbell of Glenlyon's command. Thirty-eight people were killed in the small village but many more escaped into the surrounding areas. The wife of the younger son of the chief was indeed the niece of Glenlyon.

Rob Roy MacGregor (1671-1734) was a real person, although his story has been told and retold so many times that it is difficult to know what is true and what is myth. Perhaps the most famous retelling is by Sir Walter Scott in 1817. MacGregor is buried in a churchyard in Balquhidder not far from Loch Earn.

The Auld Alliance was enacted in 1295 when Scotland, then a free nation, and France sought protection from what they both considered to be English aggression. When either Scotland or France was attacked by the English, the other country would attack some part of England's territory.

In the 15th through 17th century tapestries provided warmth against drafts and cold air while displaying the wealth of the owner. Quality tapestries were expensive because they took a great deal of time and talent to produce. The *Hunt of the Unicorn* tapestries are on display at the Cloisters, a part of the Metropolitan Museum of Art in New York. Stirling Castle in Stirling, Scotland displays replica tapestries which were woven on their property over the course of thirteen years by experts from around the world.

Acknowledgements

Even though this is a work of fiction and all people, places, and events have been fictionalized or are pure fiction, historical fiction is somewhat rooted in real events. Many thanks to the multitude of storytellers, artists, researchers, and helpful docents who put forth theories, histories and legends surrounding these times and events.

Thank you to:

Glencoe Visitor Centre and the National Trust for Scotland for educational exhibits and for protecting the natural glory of Glencoe as well as many other sites in Scotland; Historic Scotland for helping preserve many sites and cultures of Scotland including Stirling Castle, especially the Stirling Tapestries Project and its weavers; to Cloisters and the Metropolitan Museum of Art for your amazing exhibit on and displaying of the Hunt of the Unicorn tapestries; Tea Okropiridze at The Art League in Old Town Alexandria, Virginia, for teaching me the basics of the process of weaving a tapestry. All mistakes and misrepresentations in regards to such are entirely the fault of the author; and Kate Angelella for offering her editorial services as a contest prize and keeping the offer open for literally years and to her colleague Marissa Graff.

Special thanks to:

Friends and family who encouraged me throughout this project's many manifestations, including Tammy and Mary for their assistance. My nieces and nephews Sarah, Brian, Clara, Owen, Julia, Eliza and

Emily for laughing with pure joy and for enduring random, unsolicited, spontaneous history lessons.

My siblings Ruth, Paul, Paul, Elizabeth, Todd, Julia, Scott and Alanna for your love, support, and inspiration.

Mom and Dad Macreery for your continued enthusiasm and encouragement.

Mom and Daddy for instilling in me the power of family and for modeling your love of reading and history.

Team Steve for an unforgettable adventure!

Team Dave for an unforgettable adventure!

Most especially to my Rock Star husband, Bo, for his daily sacrifices, his tireless encouragement, his courageous way of approaching life, his belief in this project and his faith in us. Fight Finished. What's Next?